ALSO BY DAN GUTMAN

Baseball Card Adventures

The Genius Files

Other Novels

**And don't miss any of the books in the
My Weird School, My Weird School Daze,
My Weirder School, and My Weirdest School series!**

DAN GUTMAN

FLASHBACK FOUR

FOUR

THE HAMILTON-BURR DUEL

HARPER

An Imprint of HarperCollinsPublishers

TO NINA, SAM, AND EMMA

The author would like to acknowledge the following for use of photographs: NASA, 19; Travis Cummeau, 23; Nina Wallace, 37, 40, 99, 223, the Newberry Library, 162; Craig Provorny, 228

Library of Congress Cataloging-in-Publication Data
Names: Gutman, Dan, author.
Title: The Hamilton-Burr duel / Dan Gutman.
Description: First edition. | New York, NY : Harper, an imprint of
  HarperCollins Publishers, [2018] | Series: Flashback Four ; #4 |
  Summary: The Flashback Four are coerced by a secret government
  organization, NOYB, to travel to July 1804 Weehawken, New Jersey, to
  witness the duel between Alexander Hamilton and Aaron Burr.
Identifiers: LCCN 2018013450 | ISBN 9780062374479 (hardback)
Subjects: | CYAC: Time travel—Fiction. | Burr-Hamilton Duel, Weehawken,
  N.J., 1804—Fiction. | Burr, Aaron, 1756–1836—Fiction. | Hamilton,
  Alexander, 1757–1804—Fiction. | Photography—Fiction. | Adventure and
  adventurers—Fiction. | New Jersey—History—1775–1865—Fiction.
Classification: LCC PZ7.G9846 Ham 2018 | DDC [Fic]—dc23 LC record
  available at https://lccn.loc.gov/2018013450

Typography by Carla Weise
19 20 21 22 23   PC/LSCH   10 9 8 7 6 5 4 3 2 1
❖

First Edition

Special thanks to the kind people who helped me with this project: Rosemary Brosnan, Adam Cartwright, Kathy Crispin Cartwright, Kristin Dyan Cutler, Andrew Eliopulos, Liza Voges, Nina Wallace, and all the folks at HarperCollins Children's Books.

Pictures or it didn't happen.

—early twenty-first-century catchphrase

INTRODUCTION

THE DATE: JULY 11, 1804.

The place: Weehawken, New Jersey.

Picture this: It's early in the morning. The sun has just risen in the east. Two men stand on a flat area next to the rocky cliffs along the Hudson River. They're facing each other. Each of them has a pistol in one hand. Oh, and the guy on the left is the vice president of the United States.

Yes, you read that right. The vice president of the United States, Aaron Burr, is pointing a gun at a man. And it's not just *any* man. The gun is pointed at one of the most famous men in the world, Alexander

Hamilton. He was a major general in the Revolutionary War and the first secretary of the Treasury. He was George Washington's right-hand man. He founded the city's first bank—the Bank of New York. Even though Hamilton was never a president himself, he was a signer of the Constitution and one of the Founding Fathers of our country. If you've ever held a ten-dollar bill, you've seen his face.

Pretend you're watching a movie in your head. Hamilton and Burr are ten steps away from each other. They've been bitter rivals for fifteen years, ever since our country was born. Finally, their hatred has boiled up to the point where they've agreed to a duel to decide once and for all which one should live and which one should die.

Another man is there also. His name is Nathaniel Pendleton. He is acting sort of as a referee.

"Are you ready?" Pendleton shouted loud enough so both men could hear him.

"Present," said Alexander Hamilton.

"Present," said Aaron Burr.

According to the rules of dueling (and yes, there *were* rules for duels), each man could now fire at will. Hamilton and Burr put their fingers on their triggers and aimed their pistols. One of them was about to get shot.

Oh, before we go any further, there's just one thing I forgot to mention, reader. Four other people witnessed the scene at Weehawken that morning.

GOOD NEWS
AND BAD NEWS

EVERY STORY MUST START AT THE BEGINNING, OF course. As the old song goes, it's a very good place to start.

To tell this story correctly, we need to go back— well, actually *forward* in time. Forward to the present day. And we need to go to a specific place—Boston, Massachusetts.

Think of two boys and two girls. They're all twelve years old and in sixth grade, but they go to separate schools. Until recently, these kids didn't know one another.

David Williams is tall, thin, and African American.

Isabel Alvarez comes from the Dominican Republic. Luke Borowicz is a white kid with mild ADD. Julia Brennan is blonde and goes to the very expensive, all-girls Winsor School. Reader, I'm not trying to be all politically correct or multicultural here. It just worked out that way. They call themselves the Flashback Four.

If that name sounds familiar, it's probably because you've read *Flashback Four: The Lincoln Project* or *Flashback Four: The Titanic Mission* or *Flashback Four: The Pompeii Disaster.* If you haven't read those books, it's okay. You'll still enjoy this one. You really should read the first three, though. If you *have* read them, even better.

But just in case this is all new to you, a little background information is in order: David, Isabel, Luke, and Julia were recruited by a billionaire named Chris Zandergoth, usually known as Miss Z. In her younger days, Miss Z dropped out of Stanford University and made a fortune by creating an online dating service called Findamate. It was so successful because she figured out a way to hack into the computers of the NSA (National Security Agency), which collects emails, texts, and lots of other information about every man, woman, and child in America. Using a very sophisticated algorithm, Findamate made it easy to match up compatible people. The NSA never even knew their network had been broken into. Either that, or they decided to keep it quiet to avoid public humiliation. Hackers don't like getting hacked.

You would think that starting a hugely successful dating site, making billions of dollars, and bringing together lots of happy couples would have been enough to make Miss Z feel satisfied with her life. But she wasn't. So she spent a big chunk of her Findamate fortune—billions of dollars—to create a super-sophisticated, high-tech, state-of-the-art smartboard. You know the smartboards you have in your school? Well, this one makes those smartboards look like dumbboards. It's a *smarter* board. Why? Because it functions as a time-traveling mechanism. It's called, simply, the Board.

Go ahead, laugh. You've seen it before. You saw that movie *Back to the Future*. You've seen countless TV shows about people who traveled through time. But this thing *works*. Don't ask me to explain how. Don't even try to understand the technology. It's for super techies. With the Board, it's possible to input any date, time, place, and *voilà*—the person standing in front of it will be sent there. It *works*. You're going to have to trust me on this one, reader.

Why would Miss Z invest her fortune in such a crazy device? Simple. She has two passions in life—history and photography. After developing the Board, she recruited the Flashback Four to travel back in time and shoot photographs of historical events that were not photographed when they first took place.

For instance, Abraham Lincoln delivering the Gettysburg Address. There's no photo of it. There were photographers there that day, but Lincoln was finished in two minutes, and the photographers didn't have time to set up their cameras.

Another example—the *Titanic*. There's no photo of it sinking. One more—Mount Vesuvius as it was erupting, just before it buried the city of Pompeii in rock and ash. Photography didn't even *exist* when *that* happened. So Miss Z sent the Flashback Four back to the year 79 to take that picture.

Those missions weren't easy. Luke, David, Isabel, and Julia experienced things that no kid should ever have to live through. They were almost blown up by a live bomb. They tangled with Lincoln's assassin, John Wilkes Booth. They got arrested and thrown in jail. They were locked in a cabin on the *Titanic* and nearly went down with the ship. They were forced into *slavery* in Pompeii. The boys had to fight for their lives as gladiators. The girls had to stomp around barefoot in a tub full of human urine (it's a long story). Julia stepped in a pile of horse manure.

The Flashback Four weren't always successful in these missions. They *did* manage to get photographs of the *Titanic* sinking and Mount Vesuvius erupting. They did *not* get the shot of Lincoln giving the Gettysburg Address. But as they say, two out of three ain't bad. At least the kids survived all three missions and returned home safely. There were more than a few anxious moments in there.

If you want to learn more about what happened on those missions, read the first three Flashback Four books. I don't have time to repeat all the gory details right now. I've got *another* story to tell.

It was Friday, right after school, when the members of the Flashback Four received this text on their phones . . .

PLEASE COME TO PASTURE COMPANY ASAP

Pasture Company. That was the name Miss Z had chosen specifically for her time-travel research. The slogan was "If I don't see you in the future, I'll see you in the pasture."

It had been a few weeks since they'd gotten back

from Pompeii, and the kids were excited to hear from Miss Z again.

"Maybe she has another mission to send us on," Isabel said to herself when she received the text.

Isabel had a couple of hours to kill before she had to be home for dinner, so she took the T—the Boston subway system—downtown to 200 Clarendon Street. That's the address of the sixty-story John Hancock Tower. She punched the button on the elevator to take her to the twenty-third floor. Through the glass door up there, she could see that David, Luke, and Julia were already waiting in the reception area of Pasture Company.

The door buzzed open, and the rest of the group got up to give Isabel a big hug. After three missions, these kids had bonded as a group. They had been through a lot together, and it is not an exaggeration to say they had come to love one another.

"Where do you think Miss Z is gonna send us *this* time?" Julia asked the others.

"I want to go meet Babe Ruth," said Luke, a huge Red Sox fan. "He played for the Sox from 1914 to 1919, y'know."

"That was before they sold him to the Yankees," David added.

"Ugh," Julia said with a snort. "Baseball is such a bore. It's just a bunch of guys standing around, spitting and scratching themselves. I'd rather meet Susan B. Anthony."

"Who's *that*?" asked Luke.

"How can you not know who Susan B. Anthony was?" asked Isabel, incredulous. "She basically started the women's movement."

"Luke would only know about her if she played for the Red Sox," Julia said, cracking up the others.

The kids were so caught up in seeing one another again that at first they didn't notice a big difference in the reception area of Pasture Company. Up until now, the walls had been covered with framed photos of historical events—Neil Armstrong on the moon, Thomas Edison with his first phonograph, the Wright Brothers getting off the ground for the first time at Kitty Hawk, stuff like that. Now, oddly, all those photos were gone. The walls were blank.

Miss Z's assistant, Mrs. Ella Vader, came out and greeted the kids with her slight British accent and told them to wait five minutes. She seemed a little subdued. David picked up a copy of *Sports Illustrated* from the coffee table and leafed through it mindlessly. Finally,

Mrs. Vader ushered the Flashback Four into the main office.

The photos were gone from the walls there, too. It seemed very corporate and sterile without them. Miss Z's large wooden desk was in the middle of the room, with a small nameplate on it that said CHRIS ZANDER-GOTH. There were four chairs around the desk.

On the other side of the room was the Board. It was connected to a laptop computer on a cart. The Board itself was on wheels, so it could be moved around.

"What's going on?" asked Luke.

"Where's Miss Z?" asked Isabel.

"She'll be with you in a moment," Mrs. Vader told them quietly.

The kids took seats and glanced at one another, concerned looks on their faces. Julia mouthed the words *Something's wrong.*

Finally, Miss Z rolled in on her wheelchair. She looked to be in her forties, with a round face and dark eyes. Miss Z seemed like she was older than she had been in their previous meetings. Her hair was grayer, her face more haggard. The sparkle that had been in her eyes seemed to be missing.

"It's so good to see you kids again," she said,

smiling. "It looks like you've recovered from your adventure in Pompeii."

"We won't be going back *there* anytime soon," said Luke. "David had to fight a *tiger.*"

"Worse than that," David said, "I had to fight *you!*"

"Well, all of you did a great job," said Miss Z. "I'm so proud of you for getting that picture. I wanted to show my appreciation. Mrs. Vader?"

Mrs. Vader left the office for a moment and came back with four packages that were covered with fancy gift-wrapping paper and bows. She handed one to each of the kids. David asked if they should open them now, and Miss Z nodded.

The kids tore off the wrapping paper. Inside each package was a picture frame with the photo they'd shot of Mount Vesuvius blowing its top in the year 79. The kids had gotten out of Pompeii in the nick of time, just as tons of hot ash and rock were starting to fall on the city.

"It's *beautiful*," gushed Isabel. "Thank you!" The other three mumbled their thank-yous in agreement.

Then, the kids looked at one another. No one was sure exactly what to do next. Should they get up and leave? Should they stay and talk about the Pompeii mission? Mrs. Vader usually gave out tea and cookies, but she wasn't making a move to do that. There was an awkward silence that seemed to last forever.

"There's another reason why I asked you to come here today," said Miss Z. "I have some good news and some bad news. Would you like to hear the good news first?"

"I'd rather hear the bad news first," said Isabel. "That way we can go home with something positive."

"Okay," replied Miss Z. "Well, the bad news is that I'm dying."

THE MUSEUM OF HISTORIC PHOTOGRAPHY

O-*KAY*!

Well, *that* was awkward. What do you say when somebody has just told you she's dying? There's really no appropriate response. It's probably best to say nothing.

There was stunned silence for a few tortured moments. The kids knew that Miss Z had been suffering from ALS, amyotrophic lateral sclerosis. It's a nervous-system disease that weakens your muscles. ALS is also known as Lou Gehrig's disease, after the famous baseball player who died from it in 1941. There's no cure for ALS, and it's a progressive disease. Most people who are diagnosed with it only live between two and five years.

The Flashback Four could see that Miss Z had declined since they last saw her. But they didn't realize how advanced the disease had become. Mrs. Vader wiped a tear from her eye.

"I'm sorry," Miss Z told the group. "I didn't mean to shock you. I knew this was going to happen to me at some point. And now it has. My doctor gave me the news last week. To be perfectly blunt about it, I have a few months left. Maybe more, if I'm lucky. But statistics don't usually lie."

Miss Z had come to accept her situation, and she was quite matter-of-fact about the whole thing. That broke the tension, at least a little.

"We're so sorry," each of the kids mumbled.

"So what's the *good* news?" asked David.

"The good news," Miss Z said more cheerfully, as she pulled four embossed envelopes out of her desk drawer and handed one to each of the kids, "is that the Museum of Historic Photography is about to open!"

For much of her life, Miss Z had dreamed of building a museum and filling it with photos of the most important events in history. The museum, she hoped, would be her legacy. She didn't want to be remembered just for creating a silly dating website. So she had worked very hard over the last few years to secure a location for a museum, get the proper permits, hire an architect, and complete the necessary paperwork to turn the project from a dream into a reality. It had been a race against the clock.

"That's wonderful!" Isabel said. "Congratulations!"

"Thank you," Miss Z replied. "I knew that if I didn't make it happen fast, it wouldn't get done. You know, I have no children. After I'm gone, who knows what will happen to my estate? Even if I instructed in my will that my money should go toward building the museum, I'd have no confidence that it would ever be built. As long as I'm alive, I'm in control of where my money goes."

"So that's why all the photos are gone from the walls in here," noted Luke.

"Exactly," said Miss Z. "They're being hung at the museum as we speak. It opens one week from today. You're all invited to the ribbon-cutting ceremony, of course. It wouldn't be right if the Flashback Four wasn't there. I hope you can make it."

The kids looked at their invitations.

"It says the ribbon-cutting ceremony is black-tie," Luke said. "I don't have a black tie. Actually, I don't have *any* ties. I just borrow them from my dad."

Miss Z laughed.

"Oh, black-tie doesn't mean you actually have to *wear* a black tie," she told Luke. "You can wear whatever you'd like."

Luke was still puzzled. Why would guests be asked to wear a black tie if they didn't have to wear one? It made no sense at all. But then, except for Julia, none of the others had much experience in the strange habits of spectacularly wealthy people.

The original plan had been for Miss Z's museum to be a short walk from the National Air and Space Museum in Washington, DC. But that hadn't worked out, for various legal reasons. Miss Z had been able to acquire land on the Boston waterfront, a short walk from the Institute of Contemporary Art. She'd constructed a four-story black marble building with a large circular window poking out of the front of it, so the building looked a little like a giant camera. That was intentional, of course. A big sign on the grass out front said MOHP: THE MUSEUM OF HISTORIC PHOTOGRAPHY.

Julia, Isabel, Luke, and David arrived early, not realizing that you're supposed to show up "fashionably late" for these types of events. They were dressed in their nicest clothes, which was no problem for Julia. She always looked for an excuse to dress up. The boys looked awkward in their suits, which they'd worn for every wedding, funeral, bar mitzvah, and confirmation they had been forced to attend. David's suit was at least one size too small, as he had grown several inches in the last year.

The kids stood on the grass taking pictures and gawking as the limousines pulled up and local Boston bigwigs and celebrities got out. The kids had never seen so many rich people in one place. Some of them actually *did* wear black ties. There were news trucks too, with on-camera reporters and cameramen getting ready to go live. The place was swarming with TV, radio, and print media.

"This place is *awesome*," David said as he pulled open the front door and walked into the rotunda. Naturally, the walls were covered with historic photos, some of them blown up to huge proportions.

"I can't believe she pulled this off," said Julia.

"Hey, she pulled off the Board," David said. "Starting a museum is a piece of cake compared to that."

Many of the framed photographs on the walls were famous ones the kids had seen in Miss Z's office. An astronaut standing on the moon. The mushroom cloud created by the first atomic bomb. The Berlin Wall coming down. The Hindenburg exploding. American soldiers charging the beaches of Normandy on D-Day.

The pictures were arranged chronologically, starting with some of the first fuzzy black-and-white photos taken back in the 1800s and going all the way into the twenty-first century. People crowded around the pictures to get a closer look. Some of them took pictures of the pictures. Waiters and waitresses strolled around with trays full of hors d'oeuvres. Luke and David in particular were all over them. Free food!

After a few minutes, the crowd parted and Mrs. Vader pushed Miss Z's wheelchair into the rotunda. A hush fell over the room, and then thunderous applause rolled through the crowd as people realized who she was. Miss Z was smiling. She looked radiant in a red dress.

"Speech! Speech!" somebody hollered.

Miss Z was handed a microphone. She began to speak, haltingly at first, and then with gathering confidence.

"Thank you all for coming this evening. As many of you know, photography has been my lifelong passion. As a child, I had a darkroom in my basement, where I would spend hours developing and printing my own pictures. Those were some of the happiest days of my life.

"Back then, of course, photography was an expensive hobby. You actually had to *pay* to buy a roll of film. Remember film? Then you had to pay to have that film developed, and wait like a week for your pictures to be printed. Remember that? You had to be careful taking every shot, because every photograph cost money. Remember those days, old timers?"

Some people in the crowd nodded.

"Imagine that," somebody shouted, "a camera that did nothing but take pictures!"

"No text! No email! No Google!" hollered somebody else. "How did we survive?"

"Those were the good old days!" somebody else cracked.

"Well, I say *these* are the good old days," continued Miss Z. "Today, each of you has a camera in your pocket. I see some of you pointing them at me right now. Today you can snap a hundred pictures and blast them all over the internet instantly. It doesn't cost you a cent. You young people probably take that for granted. To me, it's simply amazing."

Miss Z was starting to feel comfortable with her words, and she continued.

"The other day I heard a young person use an expression that was new to me: 'Pictures or it didn't happen.' That's exactly right. If we don't see a photograph of an event, it's almost like that event never took place. Photographs make things real to us. Who was it that said a picture is worth a thousand words? It's true! One photo can sum up an event *instantly*. It doesn't matter what language you speak. And that moment will never be repeated, but it can be captured and saved. That's an incredibly powerful thing. Oh, I didn't mean to ramble on like this. I'm sorry. I'm supposed to be cutting a ribbon, right?"

A couple of guys brought out a thick red ribbon. They stretched it out in front of Miss Z. Somebody else brought a big pair of fake scissors and handed it to her.

"Thank you," she said, "for helping to make the Museum of Historic Photography a reality. Please enjoy this place, support it, and bring your children with you the next time you visit. Photography is a great way to teach kids about history. And it will be your children, of course, who will determine history in the future. I now declare the Museum of Historic Photography to be officially . . . open!"

With that, Miss Z cut the ribbon. There was a big round of applause.

David, Luke, Isabel, and Julia walked through all the galleries of the museum. Some of the photos and videos the kids recognized immediately. Barack Obama being sworn in as president. Several other American presidents taking the oath of office. Martin Luther King Jr. delivering his "I Have a Dream" speech at the Lincoln Memorial. For others, they had to read the plaque on the wall next to the photo to understand what it was about. Harry Truman gleefully holding up a newspaper with the headline DEWEY DEFEATS TRUMAN. The lone protester standing in front of a line of tanks at Tiananmen Square in China.

Off to the sides of the main exhibit area were smaller galleries devoted to historic photos of war, sports, poverty, crime, triumph, tragedy, heroes, and villains. Judging by the reaction of the people in attendance, the museum was a triumph.

It took about an hour for the Flashback Four to make their way through the entire museum. At the end, just before the little gift shop, they came to the final gallery. There was a black curtain in front of it and a sign that said, THE FUTURE (AND PAST) OF PHOTOGRAPHY. The kids pulled aside the curtain to see a photo on the wall. It was the picture of the *Titanic*.

COSMIC PINBALL

"LOOK, THERE'S *OUR* PICTURE!" LUKE WHISPERED as he elbowed David in the ribs. "We shot that!"

"I didn't think she was going to put it in the museum," whispered Isabel.

"Why not?" asked Julia. "That's why she sent us on the mission to shoot it."

A white card on the wall next to the picture simply said "*Titanic*, 1912" and identified the photographer as "Flashback Four." A few other people gathered around to peer at the photo. Very quickly, there was a buzz of conversation.

"I didn't know anybody took a picture of the *Titanic* as it was sinking."

"There must have been somebody in a lifeboat with a camera."

"Is this photo for real?"

"What does Flashback Four mean?"

Around the corner from the *Titanic* photo was just one more photo in the gallery—the one the kids had shot of Mount Vesuvius as it was erupting. Again, the photo credit read "Flashback Four." A larger crowd of people were gathered around the Vesuvius photo. One man was holding a magnifying glass up to it. Here, too, people were buzzing.

"Is this some kind of a *joke*?"

"Pompeii? Didn't that happen, like, thousands of years ago?"

"Photography didn't even *exist* in those days."

"This picture is photoshopped," insisted the man holding the magnifying glass. "It's a fake."

"Maybe Miss Zandergoth is trying to show us that even a photograph can't be completely trusted as authentic," a woman commented. "She's saying that photos can be manipulated. Pictures can lie. Don't you see? It's a social comment."

"It's bull is what it is," somebody else said.

"If a photo has been manipulated, it's not a real photo."

"I feel like we got ripped off," a tall man said, "and we didn't even pay to get in."

"Do fake photos belong in a museum that claims to be about historical photography?" one newscaster said into a camera. "We'll find out in our special report at eleven o'clock."

"If you ask me, this whole museum is a fraud."

The discussion was getting heated. The kids were tempted to say something in Miss Z's defense, but fortunately they didn't have to. At that moment, Mrs. Vader rolled Miss Z into the gallery. They were immediately surrounded by people peppering Miss Z with questions and reporters sticking microphones and cameras in her face. The kids moved closer so they could hear. The ribbon-cutting ceremony had turned into a spontaneous press conference. . . .

Reporters: Miss Zandergoth! Miss Zandergoth!

Mrs. Vader: Please. Back away. Miss Zandergoth is tired. It has been a long day.

Miss Z: No, it's okay. I see I've provoked some degree of controversy here.

Reporter: What's the deal with the *Titanic* photo and that one of Mount Vesuvius erupting?

Reporter: Why would you put fake photos in a museum of historical photography?

Reporter: Yeah, what are you trying to pull?

Miss Z: I'd be happy to answer your questions, if you'd just stop asking them for a moment. Just give me a chance.

Reporter: Is this a *real* museum, or Ripley's Believe It or Not!?

Miss Z: I understand your concern, and I'll try to explain. We snap a photo, and we capture that instant in time. Forever. It becomes ours. With that photo, we bring the past to us. It could be a hundred years in the past, or five minutes in the past. Either way, we get to step inside that memory and experience it as if we were—

Reporter: Will you admit that those two photos are fakes? Yes or no?

All eyes turned to Miss Z. The Flashback Four leaned forward to hear how she was going to handle the question.

Miss Z [after pausing for a moment]: They're *not*

fakes. Every photo in this museum is real. The photos have not been manipulated in any way.

There was an audible gasp.

Maybe she told the truth because she was dying and there was nothing to lose. Or maybe she just wasn't very good at lying. In any case, Miss Z had made the conscious decision to include the *Titanic* photo and the Vesuvius photo in her museum, and to tell the truth about them. She didn't seem to have anticipated the negative reaction. But now the cat was out of the bag.

"Maybe we should get out of here," whispered Isabel to the others. "We could get in trouble."

"No *way*," Julia whispered back. "*This* I gotta see."

"A photo brings a moment of time into our consciousness," Miss Z tried to explain. "So photography is a form of time travel, when you think about it. Taking a picture allows us to travel through time."

"Are you saying you figured out a way to travel through time and take pictures of events from the past?" asked one of the reporters.

All the reporters had been waiting to ask that question. It was followed by nervous laughter.

"Well . . . yes," said Miss Z.

There was another audible gasp.

"Oh my God!" Isabel whispered in Julia's ear. "She actually admitted it!"

"This is one of those times when telling the truth is *not* the right way to go," whispered Julia.

"What if she tells the truth about *us*?" asked Isabel.

"We're going to be in big trouble," Luke whispered. "I never even showed the permission forms to my mom and dad."

"Neither did I," whispered the others.

Mrs. Vader tried to pull the wheelchair away, explaining that Miss Z had to go, but Miss Z was having none of it. She wanted to talk. More members of the press and a few onlookers had gathered around. They were hanging on her every word.

"I wasn't planning to get into this today," she explained, "but since you're all so interested, the answer is yes, the photos are real. And yes, I have developed a time-traveling device."

"Why?" somebody shouted.

"Ever since H. G. Wells wrote *The Time Machine* back in 1895, people have dreamed of traveling back in time," Miss Z said. "It took over a century, but now we can do it. Now we can go back and capture images of things that were never photographed in the past.

We can find out what happened to Amelia Earhart. Now we can get a shot of General Ulysses S. Grant and Robert E. Lee signing the agreement to end the Civil War. And now we can get photographs of things that took place before photography was invented—Washington crossing the Delaware. Michelangelo painting the Sistine Chapel. The Founding Fathers signing of the Declaration of Independence. Think of it! We can go back to prehistoric times and snap a photo of a dinosaur! The possibilities are endless!"

"Are you putting us on?" one of the reporters asked. "What is this, some kind of prank TV stunt?"

"Have you had yourself examined?" asked another one. "Is there any dementia in your family?"

The crowd was turning ugly. You could feel it.

"Please, listen to me," said Miss Z. "History is like a giant jigsaw puzzle with some of the pieces missing. Finally, we can fill in those missing pieces. Isn't that a good thing?"

"Come on," said one of the guys with a video camera. "Time travel is impossible. Everybody knows that. It's just a science-fiction fantasy."

Miss Z chuckled quietly.

"You know," she said, "before the Wright Brothers got their airplane off the ground in 1903, all the experts said human flight was a science-fiction fantasy. They said it couldn't be done. But these two ordinary bicycle mechanics figured it out. And just sixty-six years later, we figured out how to send a man to the moon and bring him back safely. *That* seemed like science fiction before we did it. Who knows what we'll figure out in the future?"

"Going to the moon is a little different from going back in time, don't you think?" the guy with the video camera asked.

"Is it?" said Miss Z. "Going to the moon seems a lot *harder* to me. "I remember reading that all the experts insisted it was impossible for a human being to run a mile in less than four minutes. Like it was some kind of magical barrier that couldn't be crossed. But then, in 1954, a guy named Roger Bannister did it for the first time. Before I built what I call the Board, everyone thought time travel was an impossibility. But it's not, and these photos are the proof."

"Proof that you can photoshop anything," somebody mumbled.

"So how does this Board of yours work?" a reporter asked, a slight snicker in her voice.

"It's not easy to explain simply," Miss Z replied, "but I'll try. Einstein said nobody can travel faster than the speed of light. But he also proved that gravity could bend beams of light. So if a person can move at the speed of light on a bent light beam, certain paradoxes become possible. Space-time can warp, grow, or be collapsed. And when that happens, time is deformed too. Time is warped by the gravity of a black hole, and black holes are tunnels through the universe. If you fell into one, you would appear at another place and time. Space and time can deform enough to carry you anywhere at any speed. It's sort of like playing cosmic pinball."

"You *gotta* be kidding me," a reporter said, trying to write it all down.

"With all due respect, ma'am," said another reporter, "I think you may be off your rocker."

"They should lock her up and throw away the key," said somebody else.

"You're certainly entitled to your opinion," Miss Z said, unfazed.

"Well, if this Board of yours is so *magical*," a man with a microphone asked, "why don't you show it to us?"

"Yeah, prove it," somebody said. "Let's see it."

"I'm sorry, but I can't do that," Miss Z replied. "It took many years to develop this technology. It's proprietary. If it fell into the wrong hands . . ."

"Then why should we believe you?" somebody asked.

"I really don't care if you believe me or not," Miss Z replied.

"That's it. I'm outta here," one of the reporters said as she packed up her camera gear.

"They oughta shut this museum down right now," said another reporter.

Sadly, the story was no longer about this spectacular new museum that had opened up on the Boston waterfront. It had become a story about a nutty lady with too much money who decided to blow it all on a crazy time-travel machine before she died.

Miss Z shook her head. She had worked so hard and so long to develop the technology of the Board. She had been so careful to prepare for the missions—getting the appropriate clothes for the Flashback Four, teaching them about the language, customs, and history of the time periods they would be visiting. She thought she had covered all the bases. But something always seemed to go wrong. It was almost as if time didn't want to be tampered with.

One by one, the media left the museum to reshoot their video segments and write their stories for the next day's newspapers. Just one reporter, a short man with a beard, stayed behind. He had a pad and pen in his hands.

"So lemme get this straight before I file my story," he said, leaning over to Miss Z. "You're saying you actually traveled back in time and took those photos of Pompeii and the *Titanic*?"

"No, I did *not* say that," said Miss Z. "Now you're putting words in my mouth."

"Well, who took the photos?" he asked. "It says Flashback Four on the wall. Who is this Flashback Four?"

Isabel took a step forward. She had already opened her mouth to speak when Luke clapped his hand over it tightly.

"No!" he whispered in her ear. "If anybody finds out we were part of this, we'll be in big trouble."

Miss Z scanned the people who were still hanging around, until her gaze found Julia, Isabel, David, and Luke. She paused before speaking.

"I'm sorry, but I cannot reveal the identity of the Flashback Four at this time," she said. "That is also proprietary information."

KEEPING SECRETS

SECRETS ARE HARD TO KEEP. THAT'S WHY THEY'RE called secrets. When you know something that you know somebody else doesn't know, it's really tough to pretend you don't know! And it's even harder to keep a secret when it's so easy to just click that SEND button.

After the ribbon-cutting ceremony at the Museum of Historical Photography, Luke, Isabel, Julia, and David went back to their regular lives—school, sports, other friends. Isabel joined a club at school called Kids Against Violence. Julia returned to the issues that matter to her—makeup, hairstyles, and clothing.

None of the Flashback Four told their parents they had attended the museum opening. None of the parents asked any tough questions about that night. But the story was all over the local news and in the Boston papers the following days. It was impossible to avoid the screaming headlines. . . .

FAKE MUSEUM OPENS AT WATERFRONT

DELUSIONAL BILLIONAIRE CLAIMS TO HAVE TIME MACHINE

CRAZY RICH LADY CLOSE TO DEATH

The kids felt terrible, of course. Those stories weren't just mean and insulting. They were lies. The Museum of Historical Photography *wasn't* a fake. The pictures were all *real*. Miss Z *wasn't* delusional or crazy. If she hadn't included that final gallery in the museum with the two photos from Pompeii and the *Titanic*, the press would have been hailing her as a great educator and humanitarian.

The one headline that was hardest to avoid was the one that shouted WHO IS FLASHBACK FOUR? People love a good mystery. When word got around that the two photos were credited to somebody called "Flashback Four," it just about set off a national manhunt.

Everybody wanted to know the identity of Flashback Four. This editorial appeared in the *Boston Tribune*. . . .

The day after that editorial appeared, Isabel, Luke, Julia, and David each received this text message at exactly the same moment . . .

PLEASE COME TO THE PC OFFICE AT 4PM TOMORROW

PC. Pasture Company. It *had* to be important. So at four o'clock the next day, all four showed up at the Hancock Building. Before the kids could go through the revolving door, Mrs. Vader met them outside. A few bored-looking photographers and video crews were hanging around the front steps.

"Come with me," Mrs. Vader whispered. "Quickly!"

The kids followed her around the back of the building, where a door led to a separate elevator that was only used for celebrities, criminals, cops, and others who don't want to deal with press people pestering them.

"What's going on?" asked Luke.

"Sorry about this cloak-and-dagger stuff," Mrs. Vader replied once they were inside. "Miss Z thinks it would be best if you were not seen by the media."

She hustled the kids upstairs and offered them tea and cookies while they waited for Miss Z to make her usual grand entrance.

Finally, she did. She looked tired. It had been a rough week for her, both physically and emotionally.

"Thank you for coming in," she told the kids. "I'm sure there are more fun things you could be doing today."

"Any time," David replied. "What is it? Is everything okay?"

"We're so sorry about what happened at the museum the other night," said Isabel. "Is there anything we can do to help?"

"Yeah, those people were really mean to you," added Julia.

"Everything is fine," Miss Z assured them. "Stuff happens. Don't worry about me. Worry about people who can't pay their rent or put food on the table. I'll be fine. If I've learned one thing in life, it's to not let stuff like this bother me. I'm more concerned about the four of *you*."

"Us?" asked Isabel. "What about us?"

"If word gets out that you're the Flashback Four and that you took those photos," said Miss Z, "things could get very difficult for you."

"Difficult?" asked David. "What do you mean?"

"I'm not exactly sure *what* I mean," Miss Z replied. "But I will promise this. I will *never* reveal your names. You can count on it. And I will *not* send you on another mission. It's just too dangerous, especially now, when I'm being watched like a hawk. I feel it's time that we put this all behind us and move on with our lives."

"What about the museum?" asked Julia.

Miss Z let out a sigh and bowed her head.

"Tomorrow," she said, "the museum will be shut down 'until further notice.' The mayor is putting out the story that I'm insane, and he's using that as an excuse to shut the museum down. Here, look at this."

She pulled a newspaper out of her desk drawer.

"Oh, that's bull," said Luke.

BOSTON INQUIRER

World - Business - Finance - Lifestyle - Travel - Sports - Weather

VOL. XXV - NO. 101955   ALL THE NEWS, ALL THE TIME $2.50

FAKE PHOTOS SINK NEW MUSEUM

BY FRANK LOVECE

BOSTON - The flashy Museum of Historical Photography opened with a bang the other day, and it will close the same way after founder Chris Zandergoth astonishingly chose to display two photos that had obviously been faked, one of which had been "taken" before the art of photography even existed.

"What could she have been thinking?" asked art critic and

"That's not fair!" Isabel said. "You've worked your whole *life* to make the museum happen!"

"The press love to build somebody up, create a new celebrity out of them, and then tear them down," Miss Z said. "I must admit, people love that story. It sells newspapers. It grabs you by the eyeballs. I know how the game works."

"It wasn't *your* fault that people freaked out at the photos," David said.

"No, it *was* my fault," Miss Z replied. "I never should have included those two photos in the museum."

"But those photos are *real*!" Luke said. "I took them myself."

"Yes, but the public isn't ready for them, I suppose," said Miss Z. "I should have given it more thought. It was a mistake, maybe the biggest mistake of my life. But it's okay. I've lived a good life. You can't win 'em all, right?"

"There must be *something* we can do," Isabel said. "What if we did a public demonstration of the Board? Then people would *have* to believe it works."

"Yeah," agreed the others.

"No," said Miss Z. "I've meddled in your lives enough. This will be our last meeting. I think it's best if we don't see each other anymore."

"What about the Board?" asked Julia. "Who's going to get it when you're . . . uh, no longer here?"

"Nobody," Miss Z told her. "I have given Mrs. Vader instructions to destroy it. If this technology should fall into the wrong hands, it could be disastrous. As it is, I feel like I'm being watched. My phone may be tapped."

"Really?" David asked. "By who?"

"I don't know," Miss Z replied. "The FBI? The CIA? The NSA? It could be anybody."

"Are you sure you're not just being paranoid?" asked Luke.

"I'm just being *careful*," Miss Z said. "I don't want

you kids to get into any trouble as a result of my mistake. So let's just pretend that none of this ever happened, shall we? Chalk it up to experience."

The kids bade a tearful good-bye to Miss Z and Mrs. Vader, who helped them sneak out the back elevator again.

So that was it. The Flashback Four were finished. They would never see Miss Z again, and they would never travel through time again. Time to move on to the next phase of life.

On Sunday night, Julia (JuliaRockStar) was at her computer, as she was most nights, tweeting, Facebooking, and chatting online with some friends from her school. . . .

MistYou: U HEAR ABOUT THAT CRAZY LADY WITH THE MUSEUM?
PartyGrl: SHE SHOULD BE IN A LOONY BIN
Hisdudeness: She's nutz.
JuliaRockStar: No she isn't
MistYou: HOW DO U KNOW SHE'S NOT INSANE?
JuliaRockStar: I just do, ok?
Hisdudeness: What? U no her?

JuliaRockStar: Yeah

MistYou: HOW?

JuliaRockStar: It's a long story. Not allowed to say.

PartyGrl: SO WHAT'S THE DEAL WITH THOSE FAKE PICTURES?

Hisdudeness: Yeah? Pompeii? Come on.

JuliaRockStar: They're not fake.

MistYou: HOW DO YOU KNOW?

JuliaRockStar: I just do.

Hisdudeness: Is she your friend?

JuliaRockStar: They're real.

MistYou: REPEAT. HOW DO YOU KNOW?

JuliaRockStar: Because I was there, okay? Me and some friends took 'em. Don't. Tell. Anybody.

MistYou: SO YOU'RE FLASHBACK FOUR???!!!

Julia didn't respond after that. She knew she had already said too much. She logged off her computer. And just to be on the safe side, she cleared her browser history and didn't send any other emails, texts, or comments for the rest of the night.

Too late. The next morning, precisely at ten o'clock, four identical Lincoln Town Cars pulled up at four Boston schools.

NONE OF YOUR BUSINESS

LUKE WAS DOING HIS BEST TO PAY ATTENTION IN Mr. Wolf's math class when an announcement came over the loudspeaker. . . .

"Mr. Wolf, please send Luke Borowicz to the office."

"Oooooh!" whispered the boy sitting behind Luke. "What did you do *now*?"

"Nothin'!" Luke replied as he got up from his seat.

"You're in trouble, man."

When he got to the office, Luke was ushered into the large conference room, where he expected to see the principal, Mrs. Weissblum. Instead, a well-dressed man was sitting alone at one end of the long table with a yellow legal pad in front of him, tapping a pencil in one hand. He had a black briefcase on the floor next to him and a serious look on his face. The guy looked like it had been years since he last cracked a smile.

"Take a seat, Luke."

"Who are you?" Luke asked before sitting down. The guy was wearing a visitor's pass, but there was no name on it.

"You can call me Agent Holland."

"Agent? What are you, with the FBI or something?"

"No. Sit down, Luke."

Luke sat down.

"What do you want?" Luke said, a certain tone in his voice.

"I just want to ask you a few questions," Agent Holland replied.

"Don't you need to have a search warrant or something like that before you can question people?" asked Luke.

"Yes, we do," Agent Holland replied. "Here it is."

He pushed a piece of paper across the table. Luke scanned it long enough to see it was written in legal-ese that would be impossible for him to understand.

He noticed his own name at the top.

"Shouldn't I have a lawyer?" asked Luke. "I don't feel comfortable with this."

"How about *I* ask the questions, Luke, and you answer them?" said Agent Holland. "For starters, are you acquainted with Miss Chris Zandergoth?"

Luke didn't reply. Agent Holland jotted a note on the pad in front of him.

"Let me put it this way," Holland said. "We *know* you're acquainted with Chris Zandergoth."

"So what?" Luke asked. "Is she a criminal?"

"We know all about what Miss Zandergoth has been doing with the Board, Luke."

"Okay," Luke said. "What does this have to do with me?"

Agent Holland put down his pencil and looked Luke in the eyes.

"I'll get to the point," he said. "Are you part of the Flashback Four?"

That took Luke by surprise. He asked himself, how did this guy track him down? Did he find Julia, Isabel, and David too? Were any laws broken? What was going to happen to him?

"I'm guessing you already know the answer to that question too," Luke replied.

"Yes, we do," Agent Holland said. "And in fact, I'm pretty sure that you were the photographer of those two photos Miss Zandergoth had on display the other night at the Museum of Historical Photography."

"What if I was?" said Luke. "Is that a crime? Did I do something wrong?"

"No, quite the opposite, actually," said Agent Holland. He put his pad and papers into his briefcase. "You did a nice job on those photos. I'd like you to come with me, Luke. We're going to take a little ride."

"This is the middle of my math class," Luke said.

"Don't worry about your class," said Agent Holland. "I'll write you a note."

Luke thought about his options. He could just sit there and hope the principal would come in and rescue him. He could punch the guy. He could make a run for it. None of those seemed like smart choices. His cell phone was in his pocket. He wondered what would happen if he called 911.

"Don't reach for your cell, Luke," advised Agent Holland. "That would be a big mistake."

In the end, Luke decided to do as Agent Holland said. He followed the man out of the office and got into the black car waiting at the curb.

Agent Holland got into the driver's seat. Before

turning on the ignition, he handed Luke a black piece of cloth.

"I'm going to ask you to wear this hood over your head, Luke," he said.

"Why?"

"Because I don't want you to know where we're going."

Well, at least the guy was honest.

David, Isabel, and Julia each had a similar experience to Luke's that morning. A black car pulled up to their schools. They were sent to the office. There was a meeting with an unsmiling man and a ride to an undisclosed location.

Each member of the Flashback Four was helped out of the car, into a building, up an elevator, and into a room. There, they were instructed to take off their hoods.

"David!" exclaimed Luke.

"Luke!" exclaimed David.

"Isabel!" exclaimed Julia.

"Julia!" exclaimed Isabel.

Isabel was crying. She had never broken a rule in her life. She had never been in any kind of trouble. She had always assumed that if she simply followed the rules and worked as hard as she possibly could, bad things would not happen to her. The others were freaked out by the experience too, but to some degree they were comforted by the fact that they were together.

"Where *are* we?" asked Julia, looking around the room.

"We couldn't have gone very far," David said. "The drive over here was only a few minutes."

"I think they know everything," said Luke, as he went over to pull on the door. It was locked. "What do you think they're going to do to us?"

"I'm afraid," Isabel whimpered. "They told me not to tell my parents anything."

"Oh yeah?" said Julia, pulling out her cell phone. "Well, I'm going to tell my dad right *now*. He works for Verizon and he'll track my phone and get his lawyer over here in a minute. These people are going to get into *so* much trouble."

Julia punched a few buttons on her cell phone to call her father, but she couldn't get through.

"I can't get a signal," she finally said.

"These walls must be lined with lead or something," said David.

"What are we gonna do?" asked Julia.

"Let's just tell them the truth," Isabel said. "I don't want to get in more trouble than we're already in."

"Look, we didn't do anything wrong," Luke insisted. "We're innocent. We can't be in trouble."

"That's what *you* think," David told his friend. As the only African American in the group, David knew what it was like to be in trouble even though he hadn't done anything wrong.

"Miss Z always told us to expect the unexpected," said Isabel. "I don't think she expected this."

A minute passed before the door opened and a woman came in. The kids were a little relieved, assuming a woman would not be as rough on them as a man.

"Good morning," the woman said. "My name is Ms. Gunner." She looked to be in her fifties, with short dark hair and a business suit. She had a briefcase. The kids, of course, would soon be calling her "the Gunner."

"My name is Isabel—"

"I know all your names already," interrupted Ms. Gunner. "I know how old you are, where you live, where you go to school, and the names of your pets. I probably know more about you than *you* know about you."

"Are you with the FBI or the CIA?" asked David.

"No."

"The NSA?" asked Julia.

"I'm with NOYB," said Ms. Gunner. "We are a top-secret organization. Even the FBI and CIA don't know we exist."

"What does NOYB stand for?" asked Luke.

"That's none of your business," Ms. Gunner replied.

"Wow," said David. "This place *is* top secret."

"Can you tell us where we are?" asked Isabel.

"Isabel, if I wanted you to know where you are," said Ms. Gunner, "I wouldn't have covered your face on the way over here."

Ms. Gunner took four sheets of paper out of her briefcase and gave one to each of the kids. Then she handed out four pens.

"Sign, please."

"We're not adults," Julia said. "Our signature isn't legally binding."

Julia's dad was a high-powered corporate executive, so she knew a thing or two about contracts and legal documents.

"It's just a formality," said Ms. Gunner.

"I don't want to get in trouble," Isabel said, signing her name. "If my parents ever found out about this . . ."

Few people enjoy conflict, least of all Isabel. She had recently decided that she was going to be a pacifist—a person who rejects all wars and violence. In her bedroom at home, she had posters of Gandhi, Martin Luther King Jr., Albert Einstein, and John Lennon on the walls.

"Are you going to torture us?" David asked, signing his paper.

"No," said Ms. Gunner. "Please calm down. You are *not* in trouble and we're *not* going to torture you. You didn't do anything wrong. You will not suffer any negative consequences, as long as you do what I tell you."

"What do you want us to do?" asked Julia.

"Before I tell you that, I need to make one thing perfectly clear," Ms. Gunner told the group. "*Nobody* must know what we are about to discuss. Not your classmates. Not your parents. You will tell nobody about this meeting today or any subsequent meetings we might have. Understand?"

"Understand," all four repeated.

"That means no tweeting, no texting, no emailing," Ms. Gunner continued. "No Facebooking, no Snapchatting, no Instagramming, or whatever silly new social media you're into this week. None of it. And no phone calling, even though I'm aware that your generation rarely talks on the phone, for reasons I'll never understand. Got it? I'm looking at *you*, Julia."

"Okay, okay. I got it," Julia said. "We'll keep our mouths shut. Now, why are we here?"

"We know about Miss Zandergoth, and we know about the Board," said Ms. Gunner. "We know that she has been sending you back in time to take photographs in the past. We know everything."

"How did you find out?" asked Julia.

"A little birdie told me," Ms. Gunner replied, smirking. "Now, listen to me and stop asking questions. If the photos you took had been fake, Miss Zandergoth would have committed fraud. But we examined the photos and found them to be authentic. The fact that time travel is now a reality has very serious national security implications. For example, after she dies—and as you know, she will die soon—the Board could fall into the hands of people who would commit evil acts. They could travel through time and tamper with the historical record. Do you see what I mean? The ramifications of this are obvious and could be disastrous for our country."

"Where is Miss Z right now?" asked Isabel.

"She is safe," said Ms. Gunner. "She's in a place where she can't hurt herself, or anyone else."

"Where?" asked David.

"She is in good hands," Ms. Gunner replied, dodging

the question. "In a hospital. Receiving the best medical care."

"What hospital?" asked Julia.

"I can't tell you that."

"So in other words, you're punishing her?" said David. "You stole her technology and you're keeping her quiet."

"It's not punishment, and we didn't steal anything," said Ms. Gunner. "For the sake of national security, we feel that we need to control this powerful technology. Sometimes, when people know they're at the end of their lives and have nothing to lose, they do foolish, dangerous things."

"Where's the Board?" asked Luke.

"It is in our possession."

"Miss Z owns that technology," said David. "She spent millions of dollars developing it. You can't just take it."

Ms. Gunner sighed and shook her head. *Kids. So naive.*

"To protect our national security," she told them, "we can do *anything* we want. I assure you, everything was done strictly by the letter of the law."

"I don't like the sound of this," Luke said, folding his arms across his chest.

"Let me ask you a question," said Ms. Gunner. "Do you have any idea how Miss Zandergoth made all her money?"

"She started that online dating service," said Julia. "Findamate."

"Right," said Ms. Gunner. "And do you know why it was more successful than any other dating service? Because she hacked into the computer network at the NSA—the National Security Agency—to gather personal data on everyone in America."

"I didn't know that," said Isabel.

"Miss Zandergoth is not so innocent," said Ms. Gunner. "She's a hacker, no different from a teenage kid who plants a virus to disrupt a computer network or a country that tries to influence an election. And let me tell you, the United States government doesn't like it when people hack into government computers."

"So you just want to get back at Miss Z?" asked David. "Why don't you leave her alone? She never hurt anybody by hacking those computers."

"She *helped* people," added Isabel.

"And she has ALS," said Julia. "It's incurable. She doesn't have long to live."

"I know that," said Ms. Gunner. "At NOYB, we do not do things out of spite. Our concern is the health of our national security, not the health of one individual."

"Okay, then get to the point," said Luke, whose attention was starting to wander. "Why are we here?"

"You traveled back in time," Ms. Gunner said. "You actually witnessed Abraham Lincoln giving the Gettysburg Address. You witnessed the *Titanic* as it was sinking. You witnessed Mount Vesuvius as it was erupting."

"We did," said Isabel.

Ms. Gunner paused for a moment to imagine those things. There was just a hint of wonder in her eyes.

"NOYB wants to send you on a mission," she said.

"What?" asked Luke. "You want us to go on a mission for *you*?"

"What are you gonna do," asked David, "send us back in time to kill Hitler or something?"

"We would never ask children to assassinate anyone," said Ms. Gunner. "Not even Hitler."

"How about sending us on an *important* mission?" suggested David. "Like, send us back to 1963 to find out who *really* shot President Kennedy."

"We already know who really shot JFK," Ms. Gunner said matter-of-factly.

"Who?" all the kids asked.

"That's none of your business."

"Why did you choose us?" asked Isabel. "You could send *anybody* on a mission."

"There are a number of reasons why we've chosen you four," Ms. Gunner told them. "You have experience at this. You've done it three times now. You know how the Board works, and you know what to expect. We don't have to train you. Plus, by sending *you* on a mission, we can keep the circle of people who know about this technology as small as possible. People tend to gab to their friends, as you are well aware."

"Wait a minute," Luke said. "Miss Z was *nice* to us. She *invited* us to help her. You basically kidnapped us. Why should we play ball with you?"

"That's what I was thinking," David agreed. "What's in it for *us*?"

"Yeah, why should we cooperate with you?" asked Julia. "We could go to the press and blow the whistle on your whole operation if we want to."

"What are you going to do if we don't cooperate," asked Luke, "throw us in jail?"

Ms. Gunner sat back in her chair for a moment. Working with kids was new to her. She enjoyed their innocence.

"We prefer to use rewards rather than punishments," she told them. "It's more effective. You would be amazed to see what a rat in a maze will do to earn a reward."

"We're not rats," said David.

"Are you talking about a *cash* reward?" asked Luke. "How much money are we talking about?"

"There's no cash reward," said Ms. Gunner. "And I'll admit it, I'm not going to be as nice to you as Miss Zandergoth was. But I can offer you a tangible award."

"What does 'tangible' mean?" asked Luke.

"It means that five years from now, when you're ready, we can get each of you into the college of your choice," said Ms. Gunner. "You won't have to fill out any applications or write any essays. Oh, and there will be no tuition. You'll get a free ride to college."

"You can *do* that?" Isabel asked, her eyes open wide.

"Like that," Ms. Gunner said, snapping her fingers. "That is, we can do it if you complete the mission. If the mission is not completed, you receive nothing, of course."

Isabel was thrilled beyond words. She knew that a four-year degree at a good college would cost in the neighborhood of $250,000 or more. Her parents didn't have that kind of money. They would have to take out loans and she would have to fight to earn scholarships to pay for college.

David had been hoping that he might qualify for an athletic scholarship someday. But he realized college sports are very competitive, and only the best of the best get scholarships. A free ride would be fantastic.

Julia was not overly impressed by Ms. Gunner's offer. She figured that she would get into college anyway. Her parents had both gone to Ivy League schools. They donated a ton of money to their schools, and a building at Princeton had their name on it. So she would most likely get into college easily, and her parents would pay the tuition.

"What if I don't *want* to go to college?" Luke asked. "Maybe I want to become a mechanic and fix cars. You don't need to go to college to do that."

"I understand," said Ms. Gunner. "College isn't for everybody. You're free to leave right now if you choose, Luke. I believe Julia, David, and Isabel will be sufficient for the mission we have in mind. They can change their name to the Flashback Three."

"No!" shouted Julia, David, and Isabel.

"We need you, dude!" David told Luke. "You and me are a team. We might have to do some serious butt kicking again. Like we did in Gettysburg and Pompeii, remember?"

Luke smiled. He remembered when he and David had beaten up John Wilkes Booth and the time they'd fought as gladiators. He had almost become addicted to the pure exhilaration of time travel. It was like the feeling you get from winning a big game or landing a sick trick on your skateboard. He wanted to feel that feeling again. And he liked being part of the group.

"Okay, okay, I'm with you," he agreed. "What's the mission?"

"Let me stress this one more time," said Ms. Gunner. "If you tell *anyone* that you are working with us, we can make life very difficult for you. For starters, we'll spread the rumor that you are insane. Usually, when we spread the word that somebody is insane, it tends to drive them insane, which only proves us right. We're very good at this, believe me. We can destroy you. Do you all swear to keep this to yourselves?"

"But my mother always tells me—" Isabel started to say, but Julia silenced her with a look.

"We swear," agreed the Flashback Four. "What's the mission?"

Ms. Gunner paused until she was sure she had their full attention.

"Tell me," she said, "what do you think of when I say the name Alexander Hamilton?"

A MYSTERY OF HISTORY

AFTER SAYING THE WORDS *ALEXANDER HAMIL-ton*, Ms. Gunner looked from Isabel's face to Julia's face to David's face to Luke's face. *Nothing*. Blank stares.

"Never heard of him," David said.

"Didn't he play for the Cubs a few years ago?" asked Luke.

"Isn't he a British fashion designer?" guessed Julia. "No, that's Alexander McQueen."

"Wasn't Alexander McQueen in the original version of that movie *The Magnificent Seven*?" asked Isabel. "My mom loved him."

"That was Steve McQueen," Luke told her.

Ms. Gunner rubbed her forehead with her fingers. This wasn't going to be as easy as she'd expected.

"Don't they teach you kids *anything* in school these days?" she asked. "Alexander Hamilton was one of our nation's most famous Founding Fathers. He was the first secretary of the Treasury. He was George Washington's aide. He started the national bank."

"Oh yeah!" said Isabel, brightening.

"That was my next guess," said Luke, clearly lying.

"Was he a president?" asked Julia.

"No!" exclaimed Ms. Gunner. "Didn't any of you see that musical *Hamilton*?"

"The tickets are really expensive," Isabel replied.

In the corner of the room was a small table. Ms. Gunner took a curled-up poster out of her briefcase and unrolled it on the table. She clicked on the desk lamp so the kids could see it better.

"Does this mean anything to you?" she asked.

The Flashback Four gathered around the table to look at the drawing.

"It's one guy shooting some other guy," said Luke.

"It's not just two random *guys*," Ms. Gunner explained. "This is one of the most famous events in American *history*. It happened in 1804. That's

Alexander Hamilton on the right getting hit, and on the left is Aaron Burr, the guy who just shot him."

"I never heard of Aaron Burr," said David. "Who's he?"

"Aaron Burr was the third vice president of the United States," Ms. Gunner told him. "He served under Thomas Jefferson."

"Wait a minute," David said. "You're telling me that the vice president of the United States shot somebody . . . while he was the vice president?"

"That's *exactly* what I'm telling you," Ms. Gunner replied.

To the reader: Actually, that would not be the last time the vice president of the United States shot somebody.

In 2006, Vice President Dick Cheney shot a friend of his while they were on a hunting trip. But that's a story for another day. Sorry for the interruption.

"You *gotta* be kidding me," David said, shaking his head.

"We covered that in social studies," Isabel said. "I forgot."

"Didn't cover it at *my* school," said Julia.

"Maybe I was absent that day," said Luke.

Actually, Luke was *not* absent that day. He just wasn't paying attention.

"Wow, and I thought politics was nasty *today*," David said. "At least politicians don't go around shooting each other."

"Where did this happen—in Washington?" asked Isabel, looking at the drawing closely.

"No, in New Jersey," Ms. Gunner told her. "The town of Weehawken. On the shore of the Hudson River, just across from Manhattan. The United States of America was just sixteen years old in 1804. A teenager, you might say. Hamilton and Burr had hated each other almost since the Constitution was ratified in 1788. Finally, Burr got so mad that he challenged Hamilton to a duel."

"A gunfight?" asked Isabel. "That was *legal*? Two people could just have a disagreement and settle it by shooting at each other? That's *insane*!"

"It *was* insane," said Ms. Gunner. "And no, it wasn't legal. But people had duels anyway. That's one of the ways they settled disputes in those days."

"Why did Hamilton and Burr hate each other so much?" asked David.

"It's a long story," Ms. Gunner replied. "You can look it up sometime if you want to. But you can complete this mission without knowing all the particulars."

"Okay, so the mission is obvious," said Luke. "You want us to go back to 1804, stop the duel, and save Hamilton's life, right?"

"Wrong," said Ms. Gunner. "We don't believe in interfering with the natural course of history."

"So you want us to go back to 1804 and take a *picture* of the duel?" guessed Isabel.

"No, I don't want you to do that, either," replied Ms. Gunner.

"Then what do you want us to do?" asked David. "What's the mission?"

"I want you to go back to 1804 and shoot a *video* of the duel."

"A video?" asked Luke. "Why?"

Ms. Gunner rolled up the drawing again and put it back in her briefcase.

"Nobody knows *exactly* what happened that morning in Weehawken," she explained. "All we know for sure is that Burr shot Hamilton, and Hamilton died the next day. But did Hamilton shoot at all? Did he shoot at Burr and miss? We don't know. And if Hamilton *did* take a shot, did his gun go off after he was hit? Or maybe he missed on purpose. And if both men fired, who fired first? How much time elapsed between shots? There's so much we don't know about this duel. It's one of those mysteries of history. A still picture will not tell us exactly what happened that morning. Only a video will."

"I don't get it," Luke said, shaking his head. "What does it matter who fired first or exactly what happened that morning? It was in 1804. That's over two hundred years ago. At this point, who cares?"

"A lot of people care," said Ms. Gunner. "Historians care, and history cares. Truth matters. We want to set the record straight so we can teach the truth. Second, this is an experiment. If you're successful shooting this video, maybe we'll send you on a more challenging mission next time."

"To kill Hitler?" David asked. "We can prevent the Holocaust!"

"Maybe Hitler," replied Ms. Gunner. "Maybe Charles Manson or Jack the Ripper."

"Wait a minute," Julia said. "I thought you didn't want to interfere with history."

"In the case of the Burr-Hamilton duel, that's true," said Ms. Gunner. "But there are a lot of very bad guys throughout history whose criminal careers we would love to sort of, uh, nip in the bud, shall we say. We could save countless lives. I think that would be a good reason to interfere with history, don't you?"

"What about the butterfly effect?" asked Isabel. "You know, a butterfly could flap its wings in California and change the course of a tornado in Kansas. What if we killed Hitler and because of that, years later, like, smallpox wipes out America?"

"That's just crazy," David told Isabel.

"We don't put much stock in the butterfly effect," Ms. Gunner told the kids. "I'd be willing to take my chances that getting rid of a mass murderer before he kills his first victim will lead to a positive outcome. But let's focus on Hamilton and Burr right now."

"I have a question," Julia asked. "Aaron Burr won the duel, right? So he obviously survived."

"That's right," said Ms. Gunner. "He lived more than thirty years after the duel."

"Well, I want a free ride to college," Julia said, "but why is it necessary for us to go on this mission? If Burr survived, he must have known exactly what happened in the duel. He knew if he shot first, and all that other stuff. Didn't he tell anybody afterward?"

"Good question," said Ms. Gunner. "Burr said that Hamilton shot first. But Burr was a known liar. It was in his interest for Hamilton to have shot first. That way he could say he shot Hamilton in self-defense. If Burr had shot first, he would have been the aggressor. He could have been accused of committing murder."

"Murder?" Isabel shouted. "It was a *duel*! *Somebody* was going to get shot!"

"Not necessarily," said Ms. Gunner. "Many duels ended with *nobody* getting hurt. Dueling was sort of a dance that men did with each other to defend their honor. It had a certain etiquette to it."

"Etiquette?" the kids all said. It's hard to wrap one's mind around the weird customs and traditions of the past.

"So there was no other witness to the duel besides Aaron Burr?" asked David.

"In fact, there were two other witnesses," Ms. Gunner replied.

"Well, if there were witnesses," said David, "they should have been able to see what happened and tell the world about it."

"They turned their backs just before any shots could be fired," said Ms. Gunner.

"What? Why?"

"It's a long story. I don't have time to get into it right now."

"One more question," Luke said. "I've never used a video camera before. I don't think any of us have. If you want to do this right, why don't you hire a professional filmmaker?"

"We considered that," Ms. Gunner said. "But professional filmmakers want their movies to be shown in theaters and seen by the public. We don't want that. The video you're going to shoot will be for a very limited audience of historians. It will probably be a few minutes long, tops. You'll do fine, Luke. You did a great job in Pompeii and on the *Titanic*. I have confidence in you."

"Okay, I'm in," said Luke, slamming his open hand

against the table. "Who's with me? This sounds like it's gonna be cool."

"If Luke's in, I'm in," said David, slapping his hand on top of Luke's.

"What the heck," said Julia, putting her hand on top of the boys' hands. "It will be an adventure. Count me in."

Everyone turned to Isabel. She was hanging back, looking down, and avoiding eye contact. It appeared as though she might have had tears in her eyes.

"What's the matter, Isabel?" asked Ms. Gunner.

"I want to go to college for free more than any of you," she said. "It would mean so much to my parents. But every time we do this, something goes wrong. We went to Gettysburg, and we ended up getting arrested and thrown in jail. Remember? We went to Pompeii, and we were forced to be slaves. We almost didn't make it back. Remember how we were all freaking out and said we'd never travel back in time again? And of course we went to the *Titanic*, and that was a disaster. We *knew* it was going to be a disaster from the start. It was the *Titanic*! But we did it anyway."

"Yeah, but we always make it back," Julia assured her friend. "We always get home safely."

"We've been lucky so far to not get killed or stuck

in the past," Isabel agreed. "But I'm afraid to push our luck. Eventually, when you keep putting yourself in danger, the odds catch up with you. What if something goes wrong this time? What if we die? What if we get stuck in 1804 and have to start our lives over again from that point? My parents will freak out."

"You're *not* going to die or get stuck in the past," Ms. Gunner told Isabel. "This mission is going to be easier than those other ones. You won't have to go on a sinking ship or be close to an active volcano. That was poor judgment on the part of Miss Zandergoth, if you ask me. I promise we'll get you in there to shoot the video, and then get you out. That's it. Nothing is going to go wrong this time."

"But what if it *does*?" asked Isabel. "The NOYB doesn't care about us. Not the way Miss Z did. She rescued us when we were stuck in 1912 after the *Titanic* mission. Are you going to rescue us if we get in trouble in 1804?"

"Of course," Ms. Gunner said. "You can count on us."

"We'll take care of you, Isabel," said David.

"We've got your back, sister," said Luke.

Isabel took a deep breath and sighed.

"Okay," she said without a whole lot of conviction. "I'll do it. For *you* guys." Isabel put her hand on top of the others.

"All right!" Luke shouted. "One for all and all for one! The Flashback Four is *back*!"

"So when are we going to do this mission?" Julia asked. "I'm going to be pretty busy with schoolwork the next few weeks."

"There's no time like the present," said Ms. Gunner.

THE HOT HEAD

"WE CAN DO THE MISSION RIGHT *NOW*," SAID MS.
Gunner as she snapped her briefcase shut. "Let's go."

"Wait, what?" the Flashback Four replied as one.

"This should take maybe an hour or so," Ms. Gunner told them. "You should be home in time for dinner.
No need to call your families."

Julia, Isabel, David, and Luke were stunned. Clearly,
Ms. Gunner and NOYB handled things differently than
Miss Z and Pasture Company.

"On our other missions, we spent a lot of time in
advance preparing," Isabel explained. "Miss Z thought
it was important for us to know how the people in the

time period talked, what they ate, their customs, and stuff like that."

"She even researched and got us clothes from each time period," explained Julia, "so we would fit in with the people we were likely to meet there."

Ms. Gunner held up her hand, as if she was a traffic cop signaling cars to stop.

"First of all," she said, "you're not going to meet *anybody* on this mission. You shouldn't have to talk to anybody or eat anything while you're in 1804. I think you can survive an hour or two without food. And because you won't be meeting anybody, nobody's going to see what you're wearing. The clothes you have on right now will be fine. The duel took place in a very remote area, early in the morning. You'll be hiding behind a tree or something while you're shooting the video."

Julia looked disappointed. She *loved* dressing up. Shopping was her favorite thing to do in the world. Nothing made her happier than trying on new clothes. The main reason she'd agreed to go on the mission was because she thought she'd get the chance to model some fancy 1804 fashions.

"Second," said Ms. Gunner, "that's just not the way we do things at NOYB. We get things done quickly, cleanly, and efficiently. We don't waste time and we don't waste money. My plan is to send you to Weehawken, have you shoot the video, and bring you back home safely. That's it. This should be a fast, smooth simple operation."

"Well, that sure makes things easier," said Luke. He never liked doing research anyway. And he *hated* having to try on clothes. Most days, he wore blue jeans and one of his many Red Sox T-shirts.

"Follow me," said Ms. Gunner.

She put her face against a small device mounted on the wall that scanned her retinas and sent a signal to a central computer to open the door. It slid open with a *whoosh*.

The kids were ushered into another room, a larger and brighter room that looked more like a science lab. A few engineers were staring intently at their computer screens. On one side of the room, away from the window, was the Board. The Flashback Four got excited just seeing it again.

"Don't you think we should at least have a little background information on Alexander Hamilton and Aaron Burr?" suggested Isabel.

"I could spend hours giving you a history lesson," replied Ms. Gunner. "But how would that help you shoot the video? You can Google it when you get back, if you choose."

"I'm beginning to like this lady," whispered David, who was not particularly fond of history lessons.

"I don't feel good about this," muttered Isabel. "We're going into this blind."

Ms. Gunner led them over to an empty desk in the corner.

"What *is* important for us to discuss is the technology you'll be needing for the mission," said Ms. Gunner. "Jones, would you come over here, please?"

A tall, nervous-looking engineer got up from his desk and sauntered over. He had thick-framed glasses and a lab coat. I don't mean to stereotype, but Jones looked just like your stereotypical geeky computer expert, right down his plastic pocket protector. And like everyone else, it seemed, he had a briefcase.

"Pleased to meet you," Jones said as he shook each child's hand awkwardly. "I'm very excited to be working with you. Now, the single most important piece of equipment, of course, is going to be your video camera."

For the Gettysburg project, Miss Z had given the Flashback Four an expensive digital camera, which was large, hard to use, and even harder to conceal.

That had turned out to be a problem and the reason why they failed to bring back a photo of Lincoln delivering the Gettysburg Address. That camera was destroyed at Gettysburg.

For the *Titanic* mission, she had given them a smaller, simpler point-and-shoot camera, which had worked out well. For the Pompeii mission, they were given a standard cell phone to use as a camera.

"You're going to like this," Jones said proudly, carefully taking something out of his briefcase. It was a little thing, about the size of a golf ball, and it had a strap around it. It looked like it would fit around somebody's head.

"Is that a GoPro camera?" Luke asked. "I have a friend who shoots sick skate videos with a GoPro."

"No, I designed this myself," Jones said. "It shoots super-high-definition digital video, and the microphone can pick up a whisper from a half mile away. I call it . . . Hot Head."

Jones seemed pleased with himself for coming up with the name Hot Head.

"Cool," said Luke. "How do you turn it on? Where's the battery?"

"That's the beauty of it," Jones replied. "You don't *have* to turn it on, and it doesn't *have* a battery. You just put it on your head. Your body heat provides the power, and this little sensor functions as an on/off switch. That's why we called it Hot Head. It sees and records everything you see, and it will hold about five minutes of video. And it's just about indestructible. Here, try it."

Luke put the Hot Head on his forehead. Jones pulled on the strap so it was snug against Luke's head. As soon as he did, a little red light went on to indicate the Hot Head was recording. An image appeared on the computer screen on the wall. When Luke turned his head to look at his friends, their image was on the screen.

"That's amazing!" said Isabel, making a funny face for the camera.

"See? There's no room for human error," Jones said. "It's idiot proof."

"Well, that should be perfect for you, Luke," teased Julia.

"The Hot Head won't be available to the general public for years," Ms. Gunner said. "We spent millions in R and D to build it."

"R and D?" asked David.

"Research and development," replied Ms. Gunner. "Please take very good care of this thing. If it should fall into the wrong hands—"

"Yeah, yeah, I know," said Luke. Everybody was always worrying about stuff falling into the wrong hands.

Jones helped take the Hot Head off Luke's head, and then he took another small device out of his briefcase and held it up proudly.

"Is that our timer?" asked David.

For the Pompeii mission, David had held a timer, which had helped the kids know when they had to get back to their meeting spot to be picked up and brought home.

"No," Jones replied. "This is your new and improved TTT."

"You won't need a timer," explained Ms. Gunner. "After you've completed the mission, just send us a text with the TTT and we'll bring you back to the present day. That way, it won't be like you have to rush to a station to catch a certain train back home. It will be more like calling for an Uber."

"Nice!" said David. These NOYB people really had their act together.

TTT stands for "text through time." Miss Z had spent a good chunk of her fortune to create a little gizmo that would enable a person from one time period to communicate with a person in another time period. Imagine—in a few years you'll be able to swap texts with your great-grandparents who died a long time ago. Or you'll be able to send a text to *yourself* in the future—and receive a reply. It's game-changing technology.

Jones handed Isabel the new TTT. It was a small black box with a flip-up case to protect the keypad.

"We reverse engineered Miss Z's TTT," said Jones.

"What does that mean?" asked Isabel.

"Well, basically, we took it apart to see how it worked," said Jones. "Then we built a new one that's faster, more sophisticated, and more durable."

"On your previous missions," said Ms. Gunner, "I understand that the TTTs you were given got damaged or destroyed. But this one is made of the same material that they use to make black boxes for airplanes. So it's indestructible. Watch."

Jones took the TTT from Isabel, dropped it on the floor, and stomped on it with his foot.

"You could whack this thing with a hammer and not break it," he said, handing it back to Isabel.

"Wow!" she exclaimed.

"Use it to stay in contact with me at all times," said Ms. Gunner.

Next, Jones took a handful of coins out of his suitcase. They were old-fashioned silver dollars with a woman's profile and the word LIBERTY on them.

"You're not going to need these," Ms. Gunner explained. "But we wanted you to have some money with you, just in case of emergency."

"Where did you get these old silver dollars?" asked Julia. "They must be worth a fortune now."

"Where do you think?" said Jones, as he put them in a little cloth bag. "We coined 'em."

"Which one of you can be trusted to hold the loot?" asked Ms. Gunner.

"Me!" Julia shouted quickly. The others rolled their

eyes. If anybody knew how to handle money, it was Julia.

"Okay, I think that's all you're going to need," said Ms. Gunner as she handed the bag to Julia. "Thank you, Jones."

"Good luck," Jones told the kids before returning to his desk. "I'm very anxious to see that video when you get back. We started a pool around the office, and we're placing bets to see who shot first, Burr or Hamilton. I've got my money on Burr."

"I'm betting on Hamilton," shouted some engineer at another desk.

"Definitely Burr," shouted somebody else.

"Okay, enough chitchat," said Ms. Gunner. "Let's get going. Do you kids have any questions?"

None of the kids had any questions.

"You'll need to warm up the Board," Isabel pointed out.

"Of course," said Ms. Gunner as she went over to the Board to turn it on. "Do any of you have to use the bathroom while the Board is warming up?"

"Didn't they have bathrooms in 1804?" asked David.

"They had outhouses," Ms. Gunner told him, "and they had lots of trees."

AND AWAY WE GO

THE BOARD BUZZED GENTLY AS IT CLICKED ON and flashed some random letters and numbers to indicate it was still warming up. It takes a lot of power to transport people hundreds of years into the past.

Meanwhile, Ms. Gunner and Jones went over to a computer and opened a file titled "FB4 Project." He sat down at the desk, and she stood behind him.

"Okay," Ms. Gunner said, "let's make sure everything is a hundred percent accurate. First, set the date, Jones. July 11, 1804."

"Check," said Jones after typing that in. "Date is set."

"Set the time of day," said Ms. Gunner. "The duel took place at approximately seven o'clock in the morning. We want to give the kids time to get there before Hamilton and Burr arrive. They'll need to set up and find a good spot to shoot the video. Shall we say six o'clock?"

"Maybe we should send them earlier," said Jones, "just to be on the safe side."

"Good idea," said Ms. Gunner. "Okay, five o'clock, then."

"We have to be there at five o'clock in the morning?" complained Luke. "I don't usually wake up until seven."

"You don't have to wake up at all, dope!" Julia told him. "You're already awake! It'll be five o'clock in the morning when we get there."

"Oh, yeah," said Luke.

"Check," said Jones after typing in the time. "Time of day is set."

"Set the latitude and longitude," said Ms. Gunner. "Weehawken, New Jersey."

The coordinates for Weehawken are 40.7664° N, 74.0254° W. That means that Weehawken is exactly 40.7664 degrees north of the equator. That's the latitude. It is 74.0254 degrees west of the prime meridian.

That's the longitude. The prime meridian is an imaginary line that goes through Greenwich, England, and marks zero longitude. Every spot on earth has its own specific latitude and longitude coordinates.

"Check," said Jones after typing in all the numbers. "Latitude and longitude are set."

The screen on the Board flashed three times, and then five bands of color appeared. It was fully warmed up and ready to go.

"Okay, this is exciting!" Ms. Gunner said, clapping her hands together. "Are you as psyched as I am? Let's make some history!"

She collected the kids' cell phones, which they would have no use for in 1804. Luke and Isabel patted the pockets of their jeans. He wanted to make sure he had the Hot Head video camera, and she wanted to make sure she had the TTT. The Flashback Four went over and took their places in front of the Board.

It looked pretty much like the smartboards you have in your school, but the Board was far more sophisticated. It was packed full of highly advanced microprocessors, software, and technology way beyond anything that is available on the market today.

"Are you ready, Jones?" asked Ms. Gunner.

She looked nervous, and who could blame her?

She wasn't sending these kids down the street to pick up a carton of milk at the grocery store. She was sending them two centuries into the past to shoot a video of one of the most famous events in history.

"Ready," replied Jones.

"A few last-minute instructions," said Ms. Gunner. "I expect you kids to stick together as a group at all times. Work together as a team. Help each other out."

"We *always* stick together as a group," Luke replied. He glanced over at Julia, who had a tendency to wander off at odd moments.

David, Isabel, Luke, and Julia jammed themselves together in front of the Board. It was a tight squeeze.

"Ow, you're standing on my foot!" Isabel complained. "Get off!"

"Sorry!" replied Luke.

"Get tighter," Julia said. "If one of us has an arm or leg outside the boundary of the Board, it might get chopped off. It would be like a shark attacked us."

"We're gonna need a bigger Board," cracked David.

The Flashback Four jammed themselves together. Jones typed several commands into the computer.

"Remember," Ms. Gunner told the kids, "you are *only* going to Weehawken to shoot this video. *That* is your sole purpose. You're not going there to sightsee or bring back souvenirs. You take video, not things."

"We know the drill," Luke said, slightly irritated. "We've done this before. That's why you chose us, right?"

"I know, I know," Ms. Gunner replied. "I'm just making sure. Be careful not disturb the past in any way. You don't need to talk to anybody or interact with anything. Got it?"

"Got it," the Flashback Four said.

"Are you ready?"

"We've *been* ready," David said.

"Are you nervous?" asked Ms. Gunner. It almost seemed like she was stalling for time.

The kids weren't nervous. Well, maybe a *little*. How could you *not* be? But after going to Gettysburg, Pompeii, and the *Titanic*, the Flashback Four were now experienced time travelers. Like anything else, the more you do it, the better you get at it. They no longer needed to be told to brace themselves, or to close their eyes. They knew exactly how the Board worked and exactly what was going to happen.

"Let's light this candle," said Luke.

"Okay, do it, Jones," Ms. Gunner instructed.

Jones typed the last few commands into the computer keyboard.

"Oh, and be sure to text me every step of the way," said Ms. Gunner. "And get that video! That's the important thing. Your number one priority."

"We know, we *know*," said David wearily. "Just give it a rest already."

Jones looked up at the screen. Then he looked at the Board. Then he looked up at the screen again. He had a concerned look on his face.

"What's the matter?" asked Ms. Gunner.

"Nothing's happening," Jones finally said. "Something's wrong."

"Oh, great," said David. "It's busted."

"Serves 'em right, stealing the Board from Miss Z," muttered Julia.

Ms. Gunner and Jones put their heads together, feverishly trying to figure out what they had done wrong. They were muttering some gibberish about megabytes and warp speeds and other incomprehensible jargon, but the kids couldn't make it out. It looked like the mission would have to be scrapped.

"Did you hit the ENTER key?" shouted David.

"Oh, yeah," said Jones.

He tapped the ENTER key. There was a short buzzing sound, and then the five bands of color—red, green, blue, orange, and yellow—flashed on the Board.

"Okay, it's working!" shouted Jones. "This is it!"

"Oh, one last thing," hollered Ms. Jones as the Board flashed on and off. "Needless to say, if something should go wrong and any of you get hurt, disappear, or die, NOYB will disavow all knowledge of your existence. Do you understand that? This is *your* risk, not ours."

"Isn't it a little late to be telling us that?" shouted David.

"Better late than never," said Ms. Gunner.

"I thought you said nothing was going to go wrong!" hollered Isabel.

"Nothing *will* go wrong," said Ms. Gunner. "But if it does—"

She didn't have the chance to finish her thought. There was a flash of light and an explosion of sound. The five bands of color merged together to form one band of intense white light.

"You'd better close your eyes!" Luke shouted to Gunner and Jones. "It's about to get really bright in here."

Gunner and Jones put their hands over their faces to shield their eyes. No matter where they looked, it was like staring into the sun. They could still see the light through their eyelids.

"It's blinding!" Jones hollered.

The band of white light jumped off the Board with a sharp crackle as it stretched a few feet away from the surface, toward the Flashback Four.

Then the humming sound kicked in, a low-frequency rumbling. It sounded like a thousand people humming at the same time. The floor was vibrating. It felt like the whole building was coming apart.

"I hope we don't blow a fuse and lose power," said Jones.

The band of white light had made a connection with the Flashback Four. It was pulling them in.

"I feel it!" David yelled.

"Here we go!" yelled Luke.

One by one, the kids started flickering, like a fluorescent lightbulb that was about to blow.

"Look! It's happening!" shouted Ms. Gunner.

"Hold on!" hollered Julia.

The Flashback Four grabbed one another's shoulders for support. They had reached the point of no return. They were transitioning out of the twenty-first century and into the nineteenth.

Gunner and Jones could only stare, openmouthed.

There was one last flash of light, a puff of smoke, and the Flashback Four vanished. The noise, the lights, and the vibrations came to a crashing halt. Everything was quiet, almost peaceful.

"Wow!" Ms. Gunner said, gasping for breath. "The thing really *works*!"

CHAPTER 9

WEDNESDAY, JULY 11, 1804

ISABEL AND LUKE CRASHED INTO EACH OTHER AS they landed, bumping heads and falling down in a patch of dirt. David nearly ran into a tree. Julia tripped over a rock and stepped on something soft. It was a rat.

"Eeeek!" Julia shouted after the rat squealed to let her know it was displeased.

The rat managed to scurry away unharmed, but Julia might have been scarred for life.

"Ugh! I stepped on something that was *alive*!" she screamed. "I think it was a rat! I think I may have to throw up!"

"Shhhhhh!" said Luke. "Will you keep quiet?"

"What if there are rats all over this place?" whispered David. He was terrified of rats. But then, most people are. For some reason, people are more afraid of rats than rats are afraid of people.

The Flashback Four had landed in a small field with bushes and a few trees. There were some bottles and garbage strewn around. It seemed like a vacant lot.

"Okay, calm down," Luke said, taking charge. "First of all, is everybody okay? Any arms or legs chopped off?" He was still out of breath as he helped Isabel to her feet.

"I think I'm okay," Julia replied. "Just freaked out."

"I got a scratch on my leg," said David. "But I'm all right."

"Shhhh," Luke said. "Keep your voice down. We're not supposed to talk to anybody, remember?"

It was dark out and there were no streetlights or lights of *any* kind anywhere. Thomas Edison wouldn't be inventing the incandescent lightbulb for another seventy-five years. The sun had not reached the horizon, so there was no way to tell the time. From the light of the moon, the kids could barely make out the outlines of some buildings in the distance.

It was chilly for the month of July. The kids could hear the sound of water gently lapping on their left. It was the Hudson River.

"Okay, let's remember that this is going to be our meeting spot," Luke told the others. "After the duel is over, we need to come back here so the Gunner can bring us home. Everybody on board?"

"Yeah," said David. "And if we get separated for any reason, we'll meet up again right here. So nobody can get lost."

"Before we do anything else, I should let the Gunner know we're here," Isabel said, as she pulled the TTT out of her pocket. She opened the cover and typed a very simple one-word message on the keypad . . .

ARRIVED

She wasn't expecting a quick reply, but after a couple of seconds had passed, this appeared on the screen . . .

FANTASTIC! KEEP US POSTED.

The kids walked around the lot carefully, always on the lookout for rats or anything else that might be moving.

"This doesn't seem like a very good place for a

duel," David noted. "People may live in those buildings over there. Somebody could come out of one of them and get hit by a stray bullet."

"I can't imagine *any* place would be a good place for a duel," Isabel said. "The whole idea of shooting somebody just because you disagree with something they said seems totally stupid and immoral to me."

"For all we know, this may not *be* the dueling ground," said Julia. "Maybe Weehawken is a big town, and we're only seeing one small part of it."

They went out to the edge of the water and peered up and down the shore line. It all looked the same. There were no people in sight. They had arrived in advance of Hamilton and Burr, as planned.

"Hey, didn't the Gunner say the duel was going to take place near a cliff?" asked Isabel. "I don't see any cliff here."

Isabel was right. There was no cliff. The river came right up to the edge of the shore. There were a few rowboats tied to a small, rickety wooden pier that was a little ways upstream.

"Are you *sure* this is Weehawken?" David asked. "It doesn't look like what they were describing."

"That Jones guy punched in the latitude and

longitude for Weehawken," Luke said. "Or I assume he did. I couldn't see what he was typing."

"I wish there was somebody we could ask for directions," said Julia.

"We're not supposed to talk to anybody," Luke reminded her.

"Maybe Jones messed up," said David. "He and the Gunner didn't exactly have their act together. They didn't even know enough to hit the ENTER key."

Suddenly Luke stopped in his tracks. He was looking across the water as he pointed to the other side of the river.

"Wait a minute," he said. "Look over there!"

It was hard to see clearly in the dark, but if you squinted your eyes you could just about make out the cliffs that were directly across the river.

"*This* isn't Weehawken!" David said, perhaps a little too loudly. "*That* must be Weehawken over *there*! What are we doing over *here*?"

To the reader: You didn't *really* think the Flashback Four were going to land exactly where they expected to land, did you? We're only on chapter 9. If our story ended here, this would be a pretty short book.

Something, of course, is going to have to happen. And it will. Please be patient.

"They messed up!" Isabel said. "We're on the wrong side of the Hudson River!" You could hear the frustration in her voice. It sounded like she might cry.

"If Weehawken is over *there*, that must mean we're in New York City!" said Luke.

Everybody looked around. It certainly didn't *look* like New York City. There were no skyscrapers, no streets crowded with cars and people. But of course, this was 1804. Skyscrapers and cars hadn't been invented yet. The population of New York was around eighty thousand people. In the twenty-first century, it would be eight and a half *million*.

"Hey," David said, "we were here before. Do you remember?"

David was right. On the *Titanic* mission, after the ship sank, the kids were rescued and taken to a dock at Fourteenth Street, just about a mile south of where they were now. Of course, that was in 1912, over a hundred years in the future. A city can change a lot in a century.

David remembered from his Boy Scout days that

the sun rises in the east and sets in the west. New Jersey is west of New York. He could tell that the sun was coming up behind them. So that was proof they were in New York, and New Jersey was across the river.

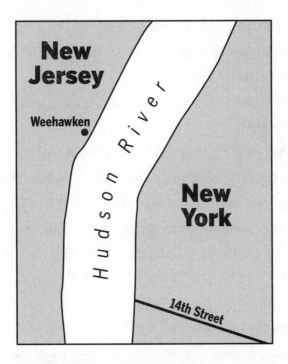

"What do you think went wrong?" asked Julia.

"Beats me," said Luke.

What went wrong, reader, is that Jones messed up the longitude. He had the latitude right—40.7664° N.

But instead of typing 74.0254 west for the longitude, Jones had typed 74.00254 west. By adding that one little zero, he had sent the kids across the river to the island of Manhattan.

"I *told* you this was a dumb idea!" Isabel said angrily. "I said something could go wrong, and it did. You wouldn't listen to me."

"Let's not start playing the blame game, okay?" David replied.

"Why not?" Isabel said, pulling out the TTT again. She was angry now. "I know who to blame. It's *them*. The Gunner and that Jones guy at NOYB. *They're* the ones who sent us here. We didn't know them from a hole in the wall. I *knew* we shouldn't have trusted them!"

She punched the keypad angrily . . .

YOU SENT US TO THE WRONG PLACE!

A response from Ms. Gunner came back quickly . . .

WHAT MAKES YOU SAY THAT?

Isabel replied . . .

NO CLIFFS HERE. WE ARE ACROSS THE RIVER IN NY!

ARE YOU SURE?

YES, WE'RE SURE!

OOPS

"Oops!" exclaimed Isabel. "All she has to say for herself is oops?"

No, that wasn't all she had to say for herself. In Boston, in the twenty-first century, Ms. Gunner was furious. She called Jones over.

"You idiot!" she shouted at him. "You punched in the wrong longitude coordinate! You messed up the whole mission!"

"What? Are you sure?" Jones asked.

"They're on the wrong side of the river!" Ms. Gunner yelled at him. "What else could have happened?"

Jones checked the computer and saw that she was right.

"I'm sorry. It was an honest mistake!" he whined. "Anybody could have done that."

"It was *not* an honest mistake!" Ms. Gunner hollered, still red in the face. "It was a careless mistake! You put those kids in danger! You might have dropped them in the middle of the river to drown! You're fired! Get out of here! Turn in your badge!"

Meanwhile, the Flashback Four were in the wrong place at the right time. Some decisions had to be made.

"What are we gonna do *now*?" asked Isabel, still on

the verge of tears.

"Let me think this through," Luke replied. "Give me a minute."

"Do we even know if this is the right *day*?" Isabel asked nobody in particular. "Maybe they got *that* wrong too."

"Man, I thought we would be able to just shoot the video and get out," David complained. "They said it was going to be an easy mission. In and out."

"They *always* say it's going to be easy," Isabel said. "Nothing is easy."

Luke hadn't come up with a solution yet.

"Wait a minute," he said suddenly, wheeling around. "Where's Julia?"

David and Isabel turned around too.

"Oh no!"

"Julia! Julia!" they began shouting.

Julia was gone.

CHAPTER 10

DESPERATE TIMES

NOW IT WAS THE FLASHBACK THREE, AND THE three were in panic mode.

"I can't *believe* she would do this to us *again*!" Luke ranted to nobody in particular.

"We were supposed to stay together as a group," fumed David.

"She *always* does this," Isabel said. "What is her problem?"

Julia did seem to have a problem with the idea of staying together with the group. At Gettysburg, she ran off and tried to steal one of the five known copies of the Gettysburg Address in Lincoln's handwriting so she could bring it home and sell it. On the *Titanic*, she ran off to grab the famous poem "Rubaiyat of Omar Khayyam" before it went down with the ship. Who knew where she'd run off to *this* time?

Somebody had to take charge, and as usual, that somebody was Luke.

"Okay, I'll go upstream and look for her," he barked. "David, you look downstream. Isabel, stay right here in case she comes back."

Luke and David ran off in opposite directions.

"Julia! Julia!" they started shouting.

It wasn't long before a voice could be heard shouting back.

"I'm right here, you dopes!"

It was Julia. The Flashback Three rushed over to where she was, near the water's edge.

"What are you doing over *here*?" David asked. "We were supposed to stay together."

"What do you *think* I'm doing?" Julia replied. "I'm getting one of these boats! How else are we going to get across the river? Come on, help me untie this rope."

Several rowboats were floating at the water's edge,

bumping gently against a dock. But before David could reply, there was a buzzing sound. It was the TTT in Isabel's pocket.

"What do they want *now*?" Isabel grumbled as she grabbed for the TTT and opened the case.

SO SORRY WE SENT YOU TO THE WRONG PLACE. NOT TO WORRY. I WILL BRING YOU BACK HOME RIGHT NOW. GO TO THE MEETING SPOT.

"Tell her to stop!" Luke hollered.

STOP

"Let's talk this over," David said.

"It was all the Gunner's fault to begin with," whined Julia. "She was the one who got us into this mess."

"It doesn't matter whose fault it was," Luke said. "We need to deal with the situation as it is now."

"Look, we came all this way," Julia said. "We're here. Why don't we just take a boat across the river to Weehawken?"

Luke and David looked across the water to try to gauge the distance to the other side of the river.

"It doesn't look that far to me," Julia said.

"All right, let's vote on it," said Luke. "All in favor of taking a boat across the river, say aye."

"Aye!" Julia said immediately. She and Luke looked at David for his vote.

"I . . . don't know how to swim," he reminded them. "You know that."

"The boat is *not* going to sink, dude!" Luke said, putting an arm around David, who appeared as though he might tear up.

"I'm . . . afraid."

"It's not like we're going to be on the *Titanic* again," Luke told his friend. "There are no icebergs out here. And you know I've got your back if you fall out of the boat."

"Are there any life jackets?" David asked.

"Come on, man!" said Luke, losing his patience. "Will you just say aye and get in the boat?"

"Aye . . . guess," David said reluctantly. "Okay, are you happy?"

Everybody looked at Isabel.

"I don't know, you guys," she said. "Can't we just go back home and try again some other time, when they can send us straight to Weehawken in the first place?"

"How do we know they won't mess up *next* time?" argued Julia. "Maybe next time they'll send us to China by accident."

"I say we're here," Luke said. "Let's go over to Wee-hawken, shoot the video, and get out of here."

"Won't it be interfering with history if we take a boat?" Isabel asked. "Remember we were told that under *no circumstances* are we supposed to interfere with history."

"How is taking a boat interfering with history?" asked Julia. "We're just getting to the place we need to be."

Isabel's brain was trying hard to come up with any possible reason why it made more sense to scrap the mission.

"Do we have time to make it across the river before the duel begins?" she asked.

"We got here two hours early," Luke said. "David and I can row fast. Let's not waste time arguing. Let's get over there ASAP, I say."

"Okay, okay," Isabel finally agreed. "Aye."

"Desperate times call for desperate measures," David said as he stepped into the boat and helped Julia aboard. "I think it was Shakespeare who said that."

Actually, reader, it was Hippocrates, the ancient Greek physician. But close enough. Back to the story.

Isabel and Luke fussed with the thick rope, trying to loosen a complicated series of knots.

"Where's the motor on this thing?" asked Julia from the rear of the boat.

"They didn't have motors in 1804!" David told her. "That's why they're called *row*boats!"

Luke and Isabel finally untied the rope that was holding the boat to the dock. Isabel climbed in carefully. Luke put one foot into the boat, and then he heard a sound coming from behind him.

"Excuse me," a man's voice said.

"Eeeeeek!" both girls screamed.

A young guy with a beard was standing on the dock, and he was holding a rifle in one hand and a lantern in the other. Luke turned around. When he caught a glimpse of the guy, he lost his balance. He almost tumbled into the river, but luckily tumbled into the boat instead, landing heavily on David.

All the members of the Flashback Four put their hands in the air instinctively. The guy looked a little crazy. He put the lantern on the ground and pointed the gun menacingly at the kids.

"Please don't shoot, mister!" shouted David. "We're just kids!"

"We didn't do anything!" Isabel yelled.

"It looks to me like you're stealin' my boat," the guy

said calmly. "*That's* doin' something."

"We're not stealing it," Julia tried to explain. "We're just . . . borrowing it."

"Hmmm," the guy said, rubbing his beard with his free hand. "Where I come from, you *ask* somebody if you can borrow somethin'. You don't just take it. Takin' without askin' is called stealin', not borrowin'."

Silence. All four kids were terrified about what might happen to them, none of them more than David. He was thinking about all the things his parents had told him that African Americans had to deal with back in what some people call "the good old days." Bigotry. Prejudice. Discrimination. Violence. David tried to make himself look invisible. Luke moved in front of him to shield David with his body.

"You're right, sir," Luke said in his most polite this-is-how-I-talk-to-grown-ups voice. "We're very sorry. May we borrow your boat?"

The guy looked Luke up and down.

"I don't reckon I know you," he said. "I don't loan my boat out to folks I don't know."

Luke leaned forward and stuck out his hand.

"My name is Luke Borowicz. I'm from Boston. What is your name?"

"Benjamin Franklin Washington," he said, shaking Luke's hand. "My parents named me after Benjamin Franklin and George Washington."

"I figured," said Luke.

"You sure are dressed funny, Luke Borowicz," said Benjamin Franklin Washington. "Why do you have that writin' on your shirt there?"

Luke looked down.

"Oh," he said. "I like the Red Sox."

Benjamin Franklin Washington looked confused.

"So why'd you write the color of yer socks on yer shirt? And why is socks spelled wrong?" he asked.

"I *knew* we should have been wearing 1804 clothes," muttered Julia under her breath.

"The Red Sox are a baseball team," Luke explained, "and they're *awesome*."

"Baseball?" asked Benjamin Franklin Washington. "What's that?"

Baseball, as we know it, would not be played in America for forty years, reader. But that's a story for another day.

"It's a game where you . . . oh, never mind," Luke said. "Look, Ben. Can I call you Ben? We're good kids. Can we just borrow your boat? We'll bring it back."

"How do I know you'll bring it back?" Benjamin Franklin Washington replied. "Maybe you'll run off with my boat and I'll never see it again. That's what the last feller did who asked to borrow my boat."

"We wouldn't do that," Luke said lamely.

Luke was out of ideas. It was time for somebody else to take over and turn on the charm.

"Ben, my name is Julia," Julia said, fluttering her eyelashes just a little. "This is one beautiful boat you have here. How much would it cost for us to *rent* it?"

"What?" Isabel whispered to Julia. "We don't have any money."

Isabel had forgotten about the silver dollars Ms. Gunner had given to them in case of emergency.

"Rent it?" said Benjamin Franklin Washington. "Well, that depends on how long you're gonna be needin' it. If you wanna take a little joyride 'cross the river, that's one thing. If you're gonna be needin' it all day, well, that's another thing entirely."

"We just want to row across the river and back," Julia explained.

"Lemme think," Benjamin Franklin Washington said. It looked like he was doing some calculations in his head.

Julia took the silver dollars out of her pocket and counted them. There were only ten. It wasn't going to be nearly enough.

"That'll be two dollars," Benjamin Franklin Washington finally said.

"Two dollars?!" Julia exclaimed. "To rent a *boat*?"

Julia's dad owned a boat, which he kept at a dock in Boston Harbor. She knew he'd paid about ten *thousand* dollars for it. It cost hundreds of dollars a month just to *dock* it.

"Okay, okay," Benjamin Franklin Washington said. "*One* dollar. But that's as low as I can go. You kids drive a hard bargain."

Julia gave him all the coins.

"Here," she said, "keep the change."

Benjamin Franklin Washington's eyes opened wide. Ten dollars was a *lot* of money in 1804. You could buy a pound of coffee for twenty-five cents in those days. For ten dollars, you could ship a ton of goods across the Atlantic Ocean to Europe.

"Tell you what," he said. "Keep the boat."

CHAPTER 11

MEANWHILE, AT HAMILTON'S HOUSE . . .

THAT EVENING HAD NOT BEEN A RESTFUL ONE for Alexander Hamilton. He knew that in a few short hours, he could very possibly be dead.

In the middle of the night, he sat at a small wooden desk doing something that he had always loved to do—write.

Hamilton was a short man, maybe five feet, seven inches tall, with reddish-brown hair that was just starting to turn gray. He had deep blue eyes and a fair complexion.

I won't bore you with his long life story, reader, but

Hamilton's was a fascinating one. He was born very poor on Nevis, a British island in the West Indies. His parents never got married, and his father walked out on the family when Alexander was ten. A few years later, his mother died. His guardian, Peter, then committed suicide, and his uncle James died a year later. Alexander was homeless. He was taken in by the parents of a friend. It was a tough way to grow up.

But Alexander was a brilliant, hardworking, and determined young man who could also be overconfident, impulsive, and arrogant at times. He came to America to go to college, and after the Boston Tea Party he joined the army to fight for American independence. By the age of twenty-one, he was a captain. He became a military leader, an aide to George Washington, and a hero at the Battle of Yorktown. He was nicknamed "the Little Lion."

When the war was over, George Washington appointed Hamilton to be the first secretary of the Treasury. He went on to start the United States Mint, the Bank of New York, and an early version of the coast guard. He signed the Constitution. Not yet fifty years old on this last night of his life, Alexander Hamilton was one of the most famous men in America.

He lived with Eliza, his wife of twenty-five years, and their seven children at the Grange, a country estate he'd built in the Harlem section of New York City. But he didn't spend this night there. He spent it nine miles to the south, in a house he rented on Cedar Street in the Wall Street area. He used it as an office, because he often had morning business in lower Manhattan. By horse-drawn carriage, it took an hour and a half to get from one home to the other. So sometimes Hamilton would spend the night at Cedar Street.

He didn't tell his wife or children about the "interview" he would be having with Aaron Burr the next morning in Weehawken, New Jersey. (That's what a duel was sometimes called in those days—an *interview*.) They would have tried to talk him out of it. But Hamilton was a careful planner, and he wanted his family to be taken care of in case he died in the duel. Ten days earlier, he had written up a statement of his finances. Two days before the duel, he wrote his last will and testament, the document that specified who would get his money and property after he died.

Hamilton's eighteen-year-old son—also named Alexander—happened to be at Cedar Street the night before the duel. At three o'clock in the morning,

Hamilton woke up his son and instructed him to go light a candle.

"Your little sister has taken ill," he told Alexander Jr. "I need you to go to the Grange to care for her."

"Cannot mother care for her?" asked his sleepy son.

"She needs your help. Go to her."

"Must I, father?"

"Be a good boy."

Hamilton didn't want his son hanging around. Not on this night. Alexander Jr. reluctantly got up, pulled on some clothes, and went to get his horse to take him to the Grange.

Alone in the upstairs study, Hamilton thought about his other son, Philip. Just three years earlier, Philip had learned that a lawyer named George Eacker had insulted his father. Angry words were exchanged. One thing led to another until—to defend his father's honor—Philip challenged Eacker to a duel. They met at Weehawken, at the same spot Hamilton would be in a few hours. In the duel, Philip was shot and killed. He was just nineteen years old. Of all the tragedy Hamilton had suffered in his life, the death of his son may have been the hardest of all.

Letter writing was a fine art in the days before email and text. Hamilton sighed as he dipped his quill into the inkwell on his desk.

By candlelight, he began to write. . . .

Statement on Impending Duel with Aaron Burr

On my expected interview with Col Burr,
I think it proper to make some remarks
explanatory of my conduct, motives and views.
I am certainly desirous of avoiding this
interview, for the most cogent reasons.

Hamilton went on to explain in four pages, point by point, why he really should *not* duel with Aaron Burr. First of all, he wrote that he was opposed to dueling, for religious and moral reasons. "It would even give me pain to be obliged to shed the blood of a fellow creature," he wrote.

Second, "My wife and Children are extremely dear to me."

Third, he wrote that he owed money to various people, and if he were to die they might not be paid.

Fourth, he wrote that he had nothing against Aaron Burr personally. They simply had political differences.

Despite all those reasons, Hamilton had decided to proceed with the duel. He had been challenged, and a man of honor must accept a challenge or be labeled a coward. That's the way it was in those days.

After that, he spelled out exactly what his strategy would be for the duel. He wrote . . .

> *I have resolved, if our interview is conducted in the usual manner, and it pleases God to give me the opportunity, to reserve and throw away my first fire, and I have thoughts even of reserving my second fire—and thus giving a double opportunity to Col Burr to pause and to reflect.*

What Hamilton was saying was that he would show up at the duel, but he would *not* try to kill Aaron Burr. He would "throw away his fire."

If you saw the musical *Hamilton* or listened to the soundtrack, you surely remember a song called "My Shot," in which Alexander Hamilton raps over and over again that "I am not throwing away my shot." But in fact, when it came time to duel with Aaron Burr, Hamilton's plan was specifically *to* throw away his shot. He even put it down on paper.

I know what you're thinking, reader. What's the

point of coming to a duel if you're not going to try to win it? Isn't that suicide?

It didn't make sense, I know. Dueling was a barbaric and strange practice, with nonsensical rules and customs. More on that later.

There was one last letter that Hamilton needed to write. He dipped his quill in the inkwell again and wrote carefully and deliberately. . . .

This letter, my very dear Eliza, will not be delivered to you, unless I shall first have terminated my earthly career; to begin, as I humbly hope from redeeming grace and divine mercy, a happy immortality.

Hamilton went on to write he could not bring himself to kill another human being. . . .

The scruples of a Christian have determined me to expose my own life to any extent rather than subject myself to the guilt of taking the life of another. This must increase my hazards and redoubles my pangs for you. But you had rather I should die innocent than live guilty.

* * *

He finished the letter by saying he wished he could have avoided participating in the duel, but he felt that he had to.

Adieu best of wives and best of Women.
Embrace all my darling Children for me.

Hamilton looked over the letter one more time to make sure he had said everything he intended to say. Then he signed it . . .

Ever yours
AH

He sprinkled some fine powder on the paper so the ink would dry quickly. Then he shook the paper for a few seconds and blew away the excess powder. He folded the letter to his wife and slipped it into an envelope. Then he dripped some wax from a candle onto the outside of the envelope to seal it, and carefully pressed his stamp into the hot wax. Finally, he slipped the letter into a thick package of other documents to be read in case he was going to die in a few hours.

There was a gentle knock on the door downstairs.

Hamilton was expecting it. He went down the steps to open the door.

Two well-dressed men were standing outside, friends of Hamilton. Nathaniel Pendleton was a veteran of the Revolutionary War and a Georgia district court judge. He was carrying a brown leather suitcase, about the size of a modern briefcase. The other man, David Hosack, was a doctor. Hosack, in fact, was also the doctor who cared for Hamilton's son after his duel. It was customary to have a doctor present at a duel. Often, a duelist would get injured but not killed.

Hamilton shook hands warmly with both men. Pendleton was courteous and dignified. He had known Hamilton since their Revolutionary War days and did not want to see his old friend risk his life over a silly disagreement with Aaron Burr.

"There is still time to reverse course, General," he told Hamilton in a soft Virginia accent. "If I may offer my advice to you, there is nothing to gain by proceeding with this altercation." Dr. Hosack agreed.

Hamilton shook his head. His mind was made up. He told Pendleton and Hosack that he planned to fire his gun into the air instead of aiming at Burr. This, he hoped, would make Burr reconsider and do the same.

That way, both men would defend their honor without either one getting hurt.

An odd strategy, I know. But it was not uncommon in the world of nineteenth-century dueling.

"Have you informed Colonel Burr of your intentions?" asked Nathaniel Pendleton.

"I have not," replied Hamilton.

"What if he should not choose to follow that same procedure?" asked Dr. Hosack.

"That, my friends, is the risk I have chosen to take," said Hamilton.

There would be no talking him out of it. Hamilton was a proud man, confident in his decisions. Up until this point, that confidence had served him well in life.

"Then it is time," said Nathaniel Pendleton, putting his hand on Hamilton's shoulder.

"Let us go," said Hamilton.

He handed Pendleton the package of documents he had written and ushered both men to the door, locking it on the way out. The three of them climbed into a horse-drawn carriage, which would take them a few blocks to the dock where a boat was waiting to ferry them across the Hudson River to Weehawken.

CHAPTER 12

OVER THE RIVER

THE FLASHBACK FOUR SETTLED INTO THE LITTLE rowboat that would take them across the river. To distribute their weight evenly, Isabel sat in the front, Julia went to the back, and David and Luke sat in the seat that went across the middle, each of the boys taking an oar.

"Okay, let's go," Julia said.

She gave a little shove, and the boat slid away from the dock. Julia waved good-bye to Benjamin Franklin Washington and promised to bring his boat back when they were done with it, even though he said they could keep it.

"Stroke . . . stroke . . . ," David said as they pulled away from Manhattan. He and Luke made a good team, having rowed a lifeboat together after escaping from the sinking *Titanic*. This one was much easier, because it was only the four of them in a smaller, lighter boat.

Isabel pulled the TTT out of her pocket.

"I'd better let the Gunner know where we are," she said, typing on the keypad . . .

WE GOT A ROWBOAT. GOING ACROSS THE RIVER.

A couple of seconds later, a reply arrived . . .

NO! LET US BRING YOU BACK HOME!

TOO LATE, Isabel texted back, WE ALREADY LEFT.

She smiled, shut the TTT case, and slipped it back in her pocket.

In Boston, Ms. Gunner slammed her fist against a table. She wasn't used to people ignoring her instructions. But there was nothing she could do about it. The kids were two hundred miles and over two centuries away. Ms. Gunner was already starting to question the wisdom of sending kids to do this mission.

Luke and David had settled into a nice rhythm, and the little boat pushed its way across the Hudson River. The water was smooth, almost like glass, because no other boats were out on the river so early in the morning. The floor of the boat was dry.

At least they didn't have to worry about getting hit by a Jet Ski, a ferry, a giant cruise ship, or an airplane landing in the middle of the river. (In fact, two hundred years later, Captain "Sully" Sullenberger would land a US Airways jet at almost this exact spot after a flock of Canadian geese flew into the engines. But that's a story for another day.)

As the boys pulled the oars through the water silently, the sun was starting to peek over the horizon. It was getting warmer. Luke and David were working up a sweat.

"Are those boats?" Isabel asked as she shielded her eyes to peer into the distant fog. "Why would anybody be out on the water this early in the morning?"

"Maybe they're fishermen," guessed Julia.

"Maybe they're Alexander Hamilton and Aaron Burr," said David.

"Come on, let's pick up the pace," Luke said. "We need to get to Weehawken before they do."

Both boys pulled harder. It doesn't *look* like it's very far across the river, but the Hudson is over a mile wide at that point. It takes almost two hours to travel that distance by rowboat, no matter how fast you're rowing. The boys were starting to get tired when the TTT buzzed in Isabel's pocket.

WHERE ARE YOU? asked Ms. Gunner.

ABOUT HALFWAY ACROSS THE RIVER, replied Isabel.

The boys kept rowing, grunting now with each stroke.

"Stroke . . . stroke . . . stroke," Julia called, trying to be helpful but really just annoying Luke and David. This was harder than they had thought it would be. Rowboats are *slow*. All four of them began to wonder whether it might have been smarter to scrap the mission as soon as they found themselves in the wrong place.

"Whose idea was it to row across the river?" David asked, not really expecting an answer.

"Not mine," said Isabel. "My idea was to go home."

It was too late to turn back now. They had to continue on. The boys were exhausted and thirsty. A little headwind picked up. In a few minutes, they were three-quarters of the way across the river.

"This is farther than I thought," Luke said, grunting loudly with each stroke.

"Do you want us to take over?" asked Isabel.

"Sure."

Crouching down to avoid tipping the boat, the

Flashback Four switched positions. Isabel and Julia took over the oars. David moved to the front and Luke went to the back.

Almost as soon as she started rowing, the TTT buzzed in Isabel's pocket. She handed it to David to answer.

WHERE ARE YOU NOW? Ms. Gunner asked.

ALMOST TO THE OTHER SIDE, David replied.

Soon they were approaching Weehawken. Looking up, the kids could see the cliffs rising in front of them. It was no wonder people came to this spot to duel. It was isolated, but also close to the hustle and bustle of New York City.

"Man, I'm hungry," said Luke, a big boy who was pretty much always hungry.

"Me too," Julia replied.

"We should have packed some Clif Bars," said David. "Get it? Clif Bars?"

"Very funny," said Julia, struggling to pull her oar through the water. "I'd eat *anything* at this point."

Finally, exhausted, Isabel and Julia steered the rowboat over to a small, sandy patch of land. They had made it to the New Jersey side of the Hudson. There were no other boats on the shore, so the Flashback Four knew they had arrived before Hamilton and Burr.

All four hopped out and slid the heavy boat behind some bushes, where it could not be easily seen.

"We made it!" Julia said triumphantly.

"What time is it?" Luke asked. "How much time do we have to get ready before the duel is supposed to start?"

He peered across the water to look at the sun, trying to estimate how high it was in the sky.

"We should have brought a watch," Isabel said.

It was ten minutes to seven.

MEANWHILE, AT BURR'S HOUSE...

AARON BURR AND ALEXANDER HAMILTON HAD SO much in common, it was almost as if they were twins.

The night before the duel, Aaron Burr was *also* up late at his desk writing letters and other documents in case it would be his last evening on Earth.

Burr spent that night just a mile and a half from Hamilton in New York City. He lived in a two-story "country home" called Richmond Hill, in what is now called Greenwich Village.

Physically, the two men were very similar. Burr was also short, about five foot six, and thin. He looked almost frail. But he was quite handsome, with dark hair and dark eyes. It has been said that he was very popular with the ladies.

Just like Alexander Hamilton, Aaron Burr had a miserable childhood. He was born in Newark, New Jersey, in 1756 (just one year after Hamilton). His father—also named Aaron—died when Aaron was a baby. A year later, Aaron's mother died. He and his sister Sally were taken in by their grandparents, but within a year both of *them* died too. Burr lost almost all his family in less than two years. Like Hamilton, he was raised by a family friend.

And like Hamilton, Aaron Burr was very smart and ambitious. He applied for admission to the College of New Jersey (now called Princeton University) when he was eleven years old. Yes, *eleven*! He didn't get in, but he was accepted a year later and graduated when he was just sixteen. Hamilton, by the way, was also rejected by the College of New Jersey.

When war broke out with England, Burr enlisted in the Continental Army. He was a Revolutionary War hero—like Hamilton. Both men fought at the Battle of Monmouth. Burr rose to the level of lieutenant colonel. And like Hamilton, he worked for George Washington.

But not for long. Washington, like a lot of people, didn't like Burr.

After the war, Burr became a lawyer in New York City—like Hamilton, of course. In fact, the two men worked together on some of the same cases. Both men had higher aspirations. Burr went on to become a New York senator, and in 1801 he became the vice president of the United States under Thomas Jefferson.

Burr and Hamilton had one other thing in common, of course. They both hated the other one's guts. But more on that later.

It was the night before the duel. Burr had spent the last few days by himself. He didn't have a big family like Hamilton did. Burr's wife had died from cancer ten years earlier, and he hadn't remarried. His adult daughter, Theodosia, lived in South Carolina. And just as Hamilton didn't tell his family about the upcoming duel, Burr didn't tell Theodosia.

What he *did* do was gather up various letters he had written or received and tie them together with a red string. Then he wrapped them in a white handkerchief and wrote a note to Theodosia instructing her to burn them. Apparently, a bunch of love letters to various girlfriends were in that stack of papers, and

Burr didn't want the whole world to know about them. Aaron Burr was a man of many secrets.

After putting his affairs in order (so to speak), Burr wrote this note to his daughter. . . .

> *I am indebted to you, my dearest Theodosia, for a very great portion of the happiness which I have enjoyed in this life. You have completely satisfied all that my heart and affections had hoped or even wished.*

Burr fell asleep on the couch in his library. Shortly after three o'clock in the morning, there was a knock on the door downstairs. It was his good friend William Van Ness, who was a federal judge in New York City. Van Ness didn't try to talk Burr out of the duel. He simply said it was time to go.

Burr hurried to put on his clothes. Even though it was the middle of the summer, he wore a black silk coat. Later, it was said that he was wearing such a heavy coat because it might help stop a bullet.

It was just six blocks from Burr's house to the Hudson River. We don't know if William Van Ness and Aaron Burr walked that distance or took a horse and carriage. We do know that a few other close friends greeted Burr when he got to the dock near Canal Street and wished him good luck. There was no telegraph, telephone, TV, or internet, of course, but word had already gotten around that there was going to be a duel that morning on the Jersey side.

A boat was waiting at the dock. It was bigger and slower than the boat the Flashback Four had purchased. Four oarsmen were sitting in it. We don't know their names. Dueling was technically illegal in both New York and New Jersey, so keeping the oarsmen anonymous would prevent them from having to testify in court about what they had seen or heard that morning.

It was about five o'clock now. Still dark out. Aaron Burr and William Van Ness stepped into the boat and took their seats. The oarsmen pushed off from the dock. They started rowing across the river and north to Weehawken.

CHAPTER 14

WEEHAWKEN

AFTER THE FLASHBACK FOUR FINISHED HIDING their boat in the bushes, they looked up. Two hundred feet above the water, the Heights of Weehawken, a part of the Hudson River Palisades, towered over them. It was a giant wall of rock. These days, people outside of New Jersey think it's a state full of decaying cities and toxic waste dumps. But Julia, Isabel, Luke, and David felt like they were standing in the wilderness, at the bottom of the Grand Canyon.

During the Revolutionary War, these high cliffs of Weehawken were used as a lookout point so the patriots could keep an eye on the British, who had occupied

New York City and controlled the Hudson River.

Weehawken was originally a word in the Lenape Indian language. There's some disagreement about what it means. Some say it's translated to be "maize land." Others say it means "place of gulls" or "rocks that look like trees" or "at the end."

In any case, the small town of Weehawken is almost directly across the river from what is now one of the most famous streets in the world—Forty-Second Street. Hamilton and Burr both left from *downtown* Manhattan, so they not only had to cross the river to New Jersey, but they also had to travel two and a half miles *upriver* to get to Weehawken. That's a lot of hard rowing.

"They're not here yet," David said, breathing a sigh of relief. He scanned the river to see if any other boats were approaching, but he couldn't tell because the early morning fog hadn't lifted yet.

"How do we know for sure that this is the right place?" Isabel asked.

"We don't," Luke replied.

There was a narrow dirt footpath leading away from the beach and up into the cliffs. Luke led the way, scrambling to climb it. There were some wispy trees and tangled brush on both sides of the path.

"Hey, check it out," David said, stopping suddenly.

He leaned over to pick some wild berries from a bush. David looked at them, smelled them, and then put one in his mouth.

"This is *good*," he said, prompting Julia and Luke to pick a few for themselves.

"Ummm," Julia said, munching a berry. "I bet *everything* tasted better back in the old days."

"How do you know those berries aren't poisonous?" asked Isabel.

"They're probably better for us than the stuff we buy in stores back home," said Luke, grabbing a handful. "No pesticides or preservatives."

"I'm *so* hungry," David said, stuffing more berries in his mouth.

"We don't have time for this, you know," Isabel told them. "Hamilton and Burr could get here any second."

"You're right," Julia said.

The Flashback Four continued climbing the narrow path until they reached a rocky ledge with a flat, grassy area behind it. It was screened by trees on all four sides. A few small boulders dotted the area, and a bunch of fallen tree branches were scattered around. The kids were about twenty feet above the Hudson.

Through the trees they could see Manhattan across the river.

"This must be it," David said. "This is the dueling ground."

David was right. In fact, eighteen duels were known to have taken place on this spot between 1798 and 1845. And there were certainly a lot more that never got mentioned in books, newspapers, or letters. The land was actually on private property, and the owner probably didn't appreciate the gunfire that was occasionally heard in his backyard. But there wasn't anything he could do about it.

The kids walked around, scoping out the area to get a sense of where the duelists were likely to position themselves. It would be important to get the right angle to shoot the video. The area was roughly rectangular, a little more than twenty paces long and ten paces wide. Off to one side, a thick tree trunk had fallen. It was lying on its side.

"This is our spot!" David shouted to the others. "We can hide behind this."

The others went over and crouched down behind the fallen tree trunk.

"It's perfect," said Julia.

Luke took the Hot Head out of his pocket and strapped it around his head. He wanted to make sure the video camera was working correctly. They all remembered what had happened at Gettysburg, when Abraham Lincoln started giving his speech and their camera suddenly went dead.

"You look like a coal miner with that thing on, dude," David told Luke, "or maybe a brain surgeon."

Luke tightened the strap so the Hot Head would be snug against his forehead, and then peeked over the tree trunk so only his eyes and the top of his head could be seen.

"Whatever I see, the camera sees," he said.

"It just turned on," noted Julia.

"How do you know?" asked Luke.

"There's a little red light on the side," Julia replied.

Luke panned his head slowly to the left and to the right. He wanted to make sure he would be filming the entire dueling ground. If just one of the duelists was in the video, it might be hard to tell who shot first. Both Hamilton and Burr would need to be in the frame at the same time.

"Okay," Luke said. "I think I'm set."

"Better take it off for now," suggested Isabel. "We could have a long wait, and that Jones guy told us the

Hot Head can only store five minutes of video."

Luke slipped the Hot Head off. The red light went out as soon as Luke's body heat was no longer providing power.

"Now we wait," David said.

"Shhhh!"

For five minutes, nobody said a word. The kids were crouched behind the fallen tree trunk, trying to stay as quiet as possible so Burr and Hamilton wouldn't notice them when they showed up. But it wasn't long before the silence became unbearable.

"I have a bad feeling about this," Isabel whispered.

"Stop worrying," David told her. "Everything's going to go according to plan. Hamilton and Burr will show up. They'll do the duel. We'll shoot the video. We'll get out of here. Simple."

"That's not it," Isabel said. "I just have a bad feeling about this whole thing. Dueling is so *stupid*. And these guys were supposedly really *smart*. They were the Founding Fathers of our country. You've got to be smart to start a country."

"They're not stupid. It was a different time," Luke whispered. "A hundred years after *we're* gone, people will be talking about all the stupid things *we* did."

That didn't make Isabel feel any better.

"Alexander Hamilton is going to *die*," she said. "Right in front of us. It feels so wrong to be part of it. I feel like I'm responsible. I wish I wasn't here."

"You're just a *witness*," Julia told her. "It's not your fault that Hamilton's going to die. It's not anybody's fault. Stuff just happens."

"Maybe we should get out of here," Isabel said suddenly, standing up. The others grabbed her and forced her back down behind the tree trunk.

"No!" David said sternly. "Do you want to get shot too when they see you?"

"I never should have agreed to this," Isabel fretted. "We were kidnapped, you know. That's what happened. It was against our will. Ms. Gunner is not a nice person. We shouldn't be working for her. It's just wrong."

"Well, you're right about that," David said. "I don't trust her. Not like I trusted Miss Z."

"Miss Z was nice," Julia said. "I miss her."

"We could mess it up, you know," Isabel said. "We could mess up the video on purpose."

"That would be wrong," Luke said. "Two wrongs don't make a right."

"Look, we made a deal to do this," David told the

others. "Maybe it was a bad deal, but it was a deal. When you make a deal, you stick with it."

Isabel continued to fret as the Flashback Four waited another five minutes. Their knees were starting to hurt from kneeling on the ground.

"What's taking them so long?" complained Julia.

"Man, I hate waiting for stuff," whispered Luke. "Waiting is boring."

"Hey, life isn't all instantaneous gratification," David said. "Sometimes you have to wait for stuff."

"Oooh, listen to *you*, with the big words," said Luke. "You gonna go to Harvard after we finish this?"

"Maybe Burr and Hamilton went somewhere else," Isabel whispered. "Maybe there's *another* dueling ground. How do we even know for sure this is Weehawken? I didn't see any sign."

"This is Weehawken," Luke said. "Just be patient."

"Hey, which one of those guys do you think is going to show up first?" asked Julia, trying to change the subject.

"I say Burr," said David.

"I say Hamilton," said Luke.

"You wanna bet?" David asked. "I'll bet you a dollar Burr shows up first."

"You're on, pal," Luke replied. "A dollar. That's the

easiest money I'll ever make. And if Hamil—"

"Shhhh!" Julia suddenly interrupted them. "What's that?"

"What's *what*?" asked Isabel.

"I heard a sound!" Julia whispered. "Somebody's coming!"

CHAPTER 15

DESPICABLE

"OKAY, NOBODY SAY A WORD," LUKE WHISPERED. "We can't let 'em know we're here."

"Shhhh!" said Julia. "Will you stop talking?"

The Flashback Four could hear the footsteps on the dirt leading up to the ledge. There was rustling in the bushes. Luke carefully slipped on the Hot Head and raised his eyes just over the top of the tree trunk so he could see and film what was about to happen.

At that moment, there was a buzz in Isabel's pocket. She grabbed for the TTT. There was a message from NOYB . . .

ARE YOU IN WEEHAWKEN YET?

Isabel hurriedly punched her reply into the keypad . . .

WILL YOU PLEASE LEAVE US ALONE? WE'RE VERY BUSY.

The footsteps were getting louder—and closer.

"Remember to hold your head steady," David advised Luke. "I hate watching shaky video."

"I know what to do," Luke replied testily. "I don't need you to tell me—"

"Shhhhh!" said Julia. "Will you two shut up?"

A man appeared on the other side of the dueling ground. Then another one. It was hard to make out their faces from that distance.

"Is that them?" asked David. "Is that Hamilton and Burr?"

"It's definitely not Hamilton," Isabel whispered. "I remember what he looks like from pictures. It must be Burr and some other guy."

"You owe me a dollar, dude," whispered David.

"Okay, okay," said Luke. "Who's the other guy?"

"Shhhhh!" whispered Julia. "Your talking is going to be on the video!"

"Your shushing is louder than our whispering!" said David.

The "other guy" was William Van Ness, who had come to Aaron Burr's house in the middle of the night to wake him up and escort him to Weehawken. In a duel, it was customary for each man to bring along a "second"—a trusted friend who would assist the duelist and make sure that the agreed-upon rules were being followed.

Burr looked pretty much the way he looked in his painted portraits. He was elegantly dressed in a long black coat, with black boots that came up so high that only a few inches of his white pants were showing. He wore a white shirt underneath, with ruffled edges at the wrists and neck. It looked like he was dressed up to go to the theater, or maybe a funeral.

Aaron Burr didn't wear a powdered wig, as some of the other Founding Fathers did. He was a thin, handsome man with dark hair that was starting to turn gray at the edges. His piercing dark eyes looked like they could burn a hole in whatever he was looking at.

The sun was rising now, and it was getting warmer. William Van Ness peeled off his jacket and started to tidy up the dueling ground. He picked up some loose branches from the area and tossed them into the woods so they wouldn't be in the way. The kids hoped and prayed that Van Ness wouldn't come over near the tree trunk they were hiding behind. While Van Ness cleaned up, Burr stood around looking impatient and fidgety.

"Hamilton is late," he muttered.

"Perhaps the general has had a change of heart," Van Ness replied.

"I always figured him to be a coward."

"He will be here," Van Ness assured his friend. "I personally delivered your last letter and put it in his hand."

A few seconds later, more sounds came from the footpath leading up to the ledge. It was Hamilton with *his* second, Nathaniel Pendleton. Pendleton was still holding the brown leather case he had brought with him to Hamilton's house. Both Pendleton and Van Ness, by the way, were wearing top hats.

Dr. Hosack, who had accompanied Pendleton across the Hudson River, did not climb up to the dueling ground. He stayed down below near the boat, for a reason. If one of the duelists should die and there was a murder trial, Dr. Hosack would be able to claim honestly in court that he had not witnessed the shooting.

"That guy on the left is definitely Hamilton," whispered Isabel.

Alexander Hamilton was more recognizable than Aaron Burr. He had a distinctive face, and of course the kids had seen it on countless ten-dollar bills.

Hamilton was also dressed quite elegantly, with a gray vest under a black buttoned coat that was oddly short in the front but went down below his knees in the back. He wore a white ascot around his neck, and his hair was neatly trimmed. Hamilton, it was said, went to the barber for a haircut every day.

He strode purposefully over to Burr. The two men were face-to-face, a couple of feet apart.

"Oh shoot," whispered David. "I think they're gonna start fighting each other right now."

They didn't. Instead, Alexander Hamilton and Aaron Burr shook hands.

"Colonel," said Hamilton, a serious look on his face.

"General," said Burr cordially.

For two guys who shared so much hatred that they were willing to kill each other, Hamilton and Burr did not show signs of anger. They looked like they had come for a business meeting.

In fact, both Hamilton and Burr had attended the same formal dinner party just seven days earlier, on the Fourth of July. At the time, neither of them had spoken a word about their upcoming duel.

And no other words were spoken as they stood facing each other on the cliffs of Weehawken. Everything had been said in advance. Further discussion was unnecessary. They knew how they felt about each other. It was time to settle their differences. At this point, their guns would do the talking.

So reader, you're probably asking the obvious question: Why did Alexander Hamilton and Aaron Burr hate each other so much? Well, there were a number of reasons.

I know some of you don't care about this kind of stuff, and that's okay. Long, drawn-out explanations can get a little dry. You want to read about the big gunfight, right?

But if you *really* want to understand what brought these two men to point guns at each other, you should read this section. People don't usually decide to risk their lives in this way unless they have a pretty good reason. But if you prefer to "cut to the chase," as they say, it's okay to skip ahead a few pages.

Hey, it's a free country, thanks to patriots like Hamilton and Burr.

The feud started back in 1791, thirteen years earlier. Aaron Burr was running for senator of New York. His opponent was Philip Schuyler, who happened to be Alexander Hamilton's father-in-law. Burr won the election. Hamilton wasn't happy.

It went downhill from there. The United States was still a very young country, and political parties were starting to form. Hamilton was a leader of the Federalist Party, which believed in a strong national government. Burr belonged to the Democratic-Republican Party (not to be confused with today's Democrats or Republicans), which feared that a strong national government could lead to a monarchy like England's. And the US had just fought a war because it didn't like the way England treated its colonies.

But really, Aaron Burr didn't have any strong political beliefs at all. And that might have been the big reason Hamilton didn't like him. Burr didn't seem to stand for *anything*. He just wanted to be rich, famous, and powerful. In Hamilton's view, he had no principles.

When Burr ran for president in 1800, Hamilton did everything he could to prevent him from winning. He even published a pamphlet saying, "You are the most unfit and dangerous man in the community." Burr came in second to Thomas Jefferson in that election, and because of the odd laws of the day, the candidate with the second highest number of votes became vice president. So Burr was "a heartbeat away" from being president of the United States.

For more than ten years, Hamilton and Burr had been throwing insults and accusations at each other, sometimes in public. Tensions built up. They came to a boil in early 1804.

Burr, knowing that his term as vice president was coming to an end, decided to run for governor of New York. Hamilton didn't disguise the fact that Burr was unfit for the job. He wrote letters calling Burr "a dangerous man and one who ought not to be trusted."

Word got around, and sometimes ended up in newspapers. Burr lost the election. Later, according to Van Ness, Burr said, "General Hamilton had at different times and upon various occasions used language and expressed opinions highly injurious to my reputation."

There was more sniping back and forth between the two of them. Then, at a dinner party in early 1804, Hamilton said some unkind words about Burr. He supposedly called him "despicable," which was just about the worst curse word you could say about another person in those days.

A doctor named Charles D. Cooper happened to be at that dinner party. He overheard what Hamilton said and wrote about it in a letter to a friend. Somehow, in

April, that letter found its way into the *Albany Register* newspaper. Burr didn't see it at first, but a friend of his showed it to him.

Burr was furious. So he did what offended people did in those days. He wrote a letter demanding to know if Hamilton had indeed used those words. Hamilton wrote back, basically saying he didn't know what Burr was talking about.

During May and June, the two men traded a number of politely worded but increasingly angry letters. Burr sent one to Hamilton demanding that he explain the "despicable" comment and demanding that he apologize for all his insults throughout their long rivalry.

Hamilton could have apologized, and that would have been the end of it. But he didn't. Hamilton considered himself to be an expert at negotiations, and he was also a very self-assured, combative man. He was incapable of apologizing for his insults, because he had said exactly what he meant.

"I trust, on more reflection," he wrote to Burr, "you will see the matter in the same light with me. If not, I can only regret the circumstance and must abide by the consequences."

In other words, bring it on. That was it. After Burr

read that letter, he'd had enough. Hamilton hadn't been particularly nice to him, but he hadn't said anything worth killing somebody over either, right? Burr thought differently. He challenged Hamilton to a duel.

So you could argue that Aaron Burr shot Alexander Hamilton over one word—*despicable*. But there was another reason why Hamilton and Burr ended up in Weehawken on July 11, 1804. And there's one more thing these two men had in common. They were both at a low point in their lives.

Hamilton had been a superstar during the Revolutionary War and afterward. He had been famous, wealthy, respected, and with his wife had a large and loving family. But his political career was in decline. The Federalists were out of power, and it didn't look like they would reclaim the presidency any time soon. Hamilton was a has-been. His hero and mentor George Washington had died in 1799.

Personally, he was depressed. After being abandoned by his own father, he'd felt responsible when his first-born son, Philip, was killed in a duel in 1802. After that, his teenage daughter Angelica had a mental breakdown. For the rest of her life, she didn't recognize her family but acted as though her brother was still alive. Hamilton's wife, Eliza, had a miscarriage. His mother-in-law had a sudden stroke and died. He was almost fifty—old for those times—and he had stomach and bowel problems.

And it didn't help that his worst enemy—Aaron Burr—was the vice president of the United States.

Burr was also in a state of personal depression. He wanted to be rich and famous. He wanted to be president. But it wasn't going to happen. He had run for president in 1796 and lost. He'd run again four years later and tied Thomas Jefferson, ending up as Jefferson's vice president. But Jefferson despised him and dropped him as vice president for his second term. Burr lost his bid to become the governor of New York. He would still be vice president for a few months. But the former war hero was now powerless and humiliated.

Personally, he was also in bad shape. He had spent a fortune and run out of money. He had no woman in his life, and his daughter had grown up and moved to South Carolina to be with her husband. Aaron Burr's future was bleak, and he blamed Hamilton, rightly or wrongly, for all his problems and disappointments.

So both men were at a low point in their lives, and

both made the foolish decision that fighting a duel might improve their situation. Now, one of them was going to die.

I know who's going to die. You know who's going to die. The Flashback Four know who's going to die. But Hamilton and Burr didn't know who was going to die.

The four men—Hamilton, Burr, Pendleton, and Van Ness—gathered together in the middle of the dueling ground.

"General," William Van Ness said to Hamilton, "let me allow you one more opportunity to apologize and explain the words you have spoken of Colonel Burr."

"I beg of you, sirs," Pendleton said to both duelists, "you can retain your dignity and walk away from this place as two honorable men."

Hamilton and Burr stared into each other's eyes for a moment as if they were trying to look into each other's souls.

"I cannot apologize for spoken words I believe to be the truth," said Hamilton.

"Then let us begin the interview," said Burr.

CHAPTER 16

RULES FOR DUELS

BEFORE WE CONTINUE WITH THE STORY, READER, a word of warning. This chapter is about dueling. Now, if you think reading about the ins and outs of dueling could possibly be boring, feel free to skip this chapter entirely. But if you think reading about dueling might be boring, you're *nuts* because dueling is *very* interesting. So stick around and read this chapter.

Unless, of course, your house is on fire right now or some other emergency is going on in your life. But if that's the case, what are you doing reading this book to begin with? You should be running to get a fire extinguisher or something.

* * *

First of all, you may think that America's Founding Fathers were one big, happy family. But in fact, they were constantly insulting one another, and many of them *hated* each other.

The Federalists hated the Republicans, and vice versa. Alexander Hamilton hated Thomas Jefferson, and John Quincy Adams called Jefferson "a slur upon the moral government of the world." His dad, John Adams, hated Benjamin Franklin. He said, "His whole life has been one continued insult to good manners and to decency."

John Adams, in fact, hated just about *everybody*. He made fun of Alexander Hamilton for being short and skinny. He called George Washington "illiterate, unlearned, unread." He had a long-running feud with Thomas Jefferson, who called Adams "a blind, bald, crippled, toothless man." And they had worked on the Declaration of Independence together!

(By the way, Adams and Jefferson died on the same day—July 4, 1826. It was the fiftieth anniversary of the United States. On his deathbed, ninety-year-old John Adams complained, "Thomas Jefferson still survives." Actually, he was wrong. Jefferson had died five hours earlier.)

Even George Washington's wife, Martha, got in on the act. She said Jefferson was "one of the most detestable of mankind."

Sometimes, these angry words turned into violence. In 1798, on the floor of the House of Representatives, Roger Griswold from Connecticut called Matthew Lyon from Vermont a "scoundrel," which was considered a curse word in its day. Lyon spit in Griswold's face. So Griswold attacked Lyon with a hickory walking stick, beating him over the head with it repeatedly. This actually *happened*! Then Lyon ran to the fireplace and fought back with a pair of iron tongs. The other representatives finally separated the two men, but a few minutes later they attacked each other again. It was like professional wrestling!

And sometimes, the angry words turned into gunplay. The idea of two grown men pointing pistols at each other because they had a little argument sounds crazy to us today. But then, so does slavery. So does prohibiting women from voting. So do any number of weird things that supposedly intelligent people did hundreds of years ago.

But lots of men (and as far as I know, they were *all* men) participated in duels in early America. It was common, especially among upper-class gentlemen and military men like Hamilton and Burr, who had seen violence with their own eyes on the battlefield.

In fact, both of these men had been involved in duels before their famous one. In 1799, Aaron Burr dueled against Hamilton's brother-in-law John Church using the same pistol he would use against Hamilton. Church shot a button off Burr's coat. And even though Alexander Hamilton didn't like dueling, he had participated in *nine* duels as a second or assistant. He was not a man to compromise, turn the other cheek, or apologize.

Most of the men who engaged in duels were not lunatics, fiends, or martyrs. So what would make two sensible, intelligent men stand twenty feet apart and point loaded guns at each other?

Sometimes it was because of an election. The loser or one of his friends would provoke a duel with the winner or one of his friends. But often, a duel would result when one guy simply insulted another guy. In those days, if you called a man a "rascal," a "scoundrel," a "liar," a "coward," or even a "puppy," you were asking for trouble. You might very well be challenged to a duel.

Two hundred years ago, if you were insulted by someone and challenged him to a duel, you were showing your courage and leadership. If you avoided the duel, you were considered to be a coward. Nobody wanted to get shot and killed, of course. But they might have been even *more* afraid of being humiliated and losing their honor. After losing the presidential election twice and then the election for New York governor, maybe Aaron Burr thought a duel with Hamilton would redeem his honor.

The other reason why men would do such a crazy thing as dueling was because they probably were *not* going to die. Most duels were not fatal. Often, shots weren't even fired. One of the duelists would apologize to the other. Or if bullets were fired, they would miss. The old flintlock pistols were not very accurate.

Sometimes the shooter would miss on purpose—fire at the ground or up in the air. That's what Hamilton said he was going to do in the letter he wrote the night before the duel. Sometimes, a duelist would aim at an arm or a leg to injure his opponent without killing him.

The point of dueling was not to demonstrate how accurately you could shoot a gun. It was to keep your honor and demonstrate your courage. It was pretty courageous to be willing to die for your honor. In fact, shooting and killing your opponent was just about the *worst* outcome of a duel—you could be indicted for murder.

Basically, dueling was a complicated and dangerous game that two men played in which they were both willing to sacrifice their life for their honor. There were even formal rules for the game. They were written down in a pamphlet titled *Code Duello*, which meant "the rules of dueling."

After you had been insulted, it was proper etiquette to write a letter to the other person demanding an apology or explanation. If the response didn't satisfy you, you would follow up with another letter challenging the man to a duel.

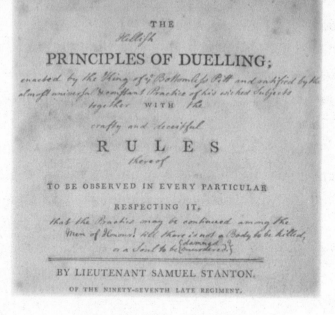

THE

Hellish

PRINCIPLES OF DUELLING;

enacted by the King of ye Bottomless Pitt and ratified by the almost universal & constant Practice of his wicked Subjects together WITH *the*

crafty and deceitful

R U L E S

thereof

TO BE OBSERVED IN EVERY PARTICULAR

RESPECTING IT.

that the Practice may be continued among the Men of Honour! till there is not a Body to be killed, or a Soul to be [damaged?] [murdered?]

BY LIEUTENANT SAMUEL STANTON,

OF THE NINETY-SEVENTH LATE REGIMENT.

After Hamilton called Burr "despicable," Burr challenged Hamilton to a duel. It would have been cowardly for Hamilton to decline, or to not show up. It would have damaged his reputation. At the same time, shooting Burr (or anyone) would have violated his moral principles. So it made sense for Hamilton to accept the duel and then "throw away his shot." It would show the world he was a man of courage, principles, and honor.

I should point out that some historians have speculated that Alexander Hamilton had a death wish. It has even been suggested that Hamilton and Burr were so much alike that their duel was a case of assisted suicide. I'll leave that to the psychologists to debate.

In any case, after the Hamilton-Burr episode, dueling fell out of favor and gradually faded away. Nowadays, people don't resolve their differences by dueling. No, today we sue each other! Instead of saying, "Meet me in Weehawken at dawn," we say, "I'll see you in court!"

But enough of this talk about dueling. Back to the duel . . .

READY . . . AIM . . .

"OKAY, GET READY," JULIA WHISPERED TO LUKE AS they crouched behind the fallen tree. "This could go very fast."

"I'm ready," Luke whispered back, his head poking just above the tree trunk.

The Flashback Four were expecting the duel to be sort of like one of those Wild West gunfights we've all seen in old movies. You know, two gunslingers face off against each other on an empty street. Terrified townspeople cower off to the side. One of the gunslingers shouts, "Draw!" Both men pull their pistols out of their holsters as fast as they can. Two gunshots ring out. The one who was a millisecond slower drops to the ground, clutching his chest in agony. The quicker one blows the smoke from the end of his barrel and calmly walks off into the sunset.

But that's not the way it happened with Hamilton and Burr. Dueling in the nineteenth century had an elaborate ceremony to it. First, the positioning of the duelists had to be determined. It went something like this. . . .

Aaron Burr's second, William Van Ness, took a pair of dice out of his pocket. He got down on one knee and shook the dice in his hand.

"Two!" called out Burr.

"Eleven!" called out Hamilton.

Van Ness rolled the dice on a patch of dirt.

"It is ten," announced Mr. Van Ness as he picked up the dice and stood. "General Hamilton will choose his position."

Hamilton looked around and leaned his head toward Nathaniel Pendleton. They whispered back and forth as they pointed in various directions.

"General Hamilton chooses north," Pendleton announced, pointing toward the side of the dueling ground that faced the river and New York City.

"Why did he choose *that* side?" whispered Luke. "Won't he have the sun in his eyes?"

"Dumb move," agreed David. "That's like a football team winning the coin toss and electing to kick off."

"Shhhhh!" whispered Julia. "Will you two quiet down? They'll hear you."

Mr. Van Ness got down on one knee again.

"Now we will determine which one of us will supervise the interview," he said, shaking the dice in his hand.

"Two!" called out Hamilton.

"Ten!" called out Burr.

Van Ness rolled the dice.

"It is three," he announced, shaking his head in dismay. "General Hamilton wins yet again. This must be your lucky day, sir."

"That remains to be seen," mumbled Aaron Burr. "The day is young."

Hamilton's second—Nathaniel Pendleton—would supervise the duel.

As the one who had been challenged, it was Alexander Hamilton's responsibility to bring the weapons to the duel. Hamilton was not a gun owner himself, but many upper-class gentlemen of the day kept a set of pistols around, if only for decoration.

Nathaniel Pendleton walked about ten feet to the side to get the brown leather case he had left on the ground. It was called a *portmanteau*. He loosened the straps and opened the case. There were two pistols inside.

"I was *wondering* what was in that case," Isabel whispered from behind the tree trunk.

The guns had been borrowed from Hamilton's brother-in-law John Barker Church. These were the same pistols that Hamilton's son Philip had used in his fatal duel three years earlier. They were made in the 1790s by a well-known London gunsmith named Wogdon. The guns had been stored in the portmanteau for a reason. If there was a trial after the duel was over, the men rowing the boats could truthfully swear under oath that they had not seen any weapons.

Reader, I must confess that I'm uncomfortable talking about guns in a book for young readers. The whole topic is a very controversial one in America, as you know. Some people believe gun ownership should be strictly controlled. Others feel we would be safer if all citizens were armed. Both sides, hopefully, agree that guns are very dangerous weapons that should not be touched without a grown-up present.

Some people may feel this whole *book* is inappropriate for children. But the Hamilton-Burr duel is a part of our history, and you should know about it.

Now, you're probably thinking that the pistols in this duel worked like the ones you've seen in movies. Six shots. Six trigger pulls. *Boom. Boom. Boom.* Like that.

In fact, the revolver—a gun that could fire six bullets from a chamber that revolved—wasn't invented until ten years after this duel. The guns Hamilton and Burr used were flintlock pistols. That meant when the trigger was pulled, a piece of steel would hit a piece of flint. That produced a spark, which created a small explosion, which sent a bullet flying through the barrel. These were much more primitive than modern pistols.

Pendleton handed one weapon to Burr and the other one to Hamilton. Neither man was wearing a holster. They just held the gun in their hands.

At that moment, there was a buzz in Isabel's pocket.

DID THE DUEL START YET? read the message on the TTT screen.

Isabel typed back, irritated . . .

CAN'T TALK THEY'RE ABOUT TO DUEL!

Aaron Burr and William Van Ness inspected their gun carefully. The barrel was close to a foot long. It looked like it would be heavy to hold up, and in fact it weighed several pounds. The handle was made from carved walnut, with fancy designs on each side. There were gold mountings along the brass barrel.

"It is acceptable," Burr said.

Alexander Hamilton seemed less interested in examining his weapon. The day before, Pendleton had come over to Hamilton's house to show him the pistols. Hamilton had simply picked one up and put it down. If he was really going to throw away his shot, the gun in his hand didn't matter much. He probably hadn't fired one since the Revolutionary War. Aaron Burr, some people said later, had been practicing his marksmanship the week before the duel.

"Acceptable," Hamilton said.

In Isabel's pocket, the TTT buzzed again.

IS THE DUEL OVER?

NO!

Next, it was Van Ness and Pendleton's job to load the weapons. Still standing next to each other, they each took a small container of black powder with sulfur in it and carefully poured a little into the barrels of their respective guns. Then they dropped one bullet— a .56-caliber lead ball that weighed an ounce—into each of the barrels. The balls were wrapped in a small piece of paper called wadding. Finally, a metal plunger called a ramrod was used to push the bullet down to the end of the barrel. This whole process took around twenty seconds.

"Those guns can only fire one bullet at a time," Luke marveled.

"They're lame," whispered David.

"Shhhhh!"

Not only were the guns incapable of shooting more than one bullet, but they weren't very accurate either. These pistols were "smoothbore," which meant the inside of the barrel was perfectly smooth. Modern guns have grooves inside the barrel, which puts a spin on the bullet. This makes it fly straighter, the same way a football flies straighter when the quarterback throws a perfect spiral pass. And you might know that these days bullets are shaped more like footballs than baseballs.

With the weapons loaded, Pendleton and Van Ness cocked the triggers with a loud click and carefully handed the guns to Hamilton and Burr.

"Would you like me to set the hair spring?" Pendleton asked Hamilton.

"Not this time," he replied.

The guns had a hair trigger, which was an optional setting that made the trigger easier to pull. Without it, a shooter needed to use twenty pounds of pressure to fire. With the hair trigger on, he only needed one pound of pressure.

Next, Pendleton and Van Ness had the job of determining where each of the duelists would be positioned. They chose a starting point in the middle of the dueling ground and marked out ten paces between them until they were about twenty feet apart. Hamilton and Burr walked over to their assigned spots.

Pendleton and Van Ness stepped off to the side so

they would be far away from the line of fire.

"This is it," Julia whispered, taking a deep breath so she could hold it.

But there was one last task for the seconds to do. Nathaniel Pendleton pulled a small pamphlet from his pocket and began to read from it. It was the *Code Duello*.

"Gentlemen," he announced loudly. "This is how we shall proceed. I will ask you if you are ready. If so, you will say the word 'present.' You may then fire your weapon when you please. If one party fires his weapon and the other does not, the gentleman who withheld fire must wait for his second to say, 'One, two, three, fire' before firing. If the opponent refuses to do so, then both duelists will confer to see if the dispute can be settled verbally or whether a second round is required."

"Huh?" Luke whispered. "Did that make any sense to you?"

"No," replied David.

"Those rules are *complicated*," whispered Isabel.

"They'll have to load the guns all over again if nobody gets hit in the first round," whispered Julia.

It may have seemed confusing to the Flashback Four, but Hamilton and Burr knew exactly what to do.

As mentioned earlier, this was not the first duel for either of them.

"Do all parties understand the rules as they have been stated?" asked Pendleton.

"I do," both duelists replied.

"Then let us commence," said Pendleton.

There was another buzz in Isabel's pocket.

HOW ABOUT NOW? it said on the screen of the TTT.

Isabel didn't even open the case to read that text this time. She wasn't about to take her eyes off the duel *now*.

. . . FIRE!

THIS WAS *IT*.

The preliminary nonsense was finished. It had all come down to this moment. The Flashback Four held their collective breath. Luke prayed that there would still be enough memory left in the Hot Head to capture the two or three crucial seconds when shots were actually fired. Beads of sweat appeared on his forehead. He was afraid to wipe them away.

Alexander Hamilton and Aaron Burr both turned their bodies sideways, the way fencers do, to make a smaller target for their opponent to hit.

"I don't want to look!" whispered Isabel, half covering her eyes.

"Are you kidding?" whispered Julia. "This is why we're here!"

"Are both parties ready?" announced Nathaniel Pendleton.

"Present," said Aaron Burr, raising his pistol.

"Stop," said Hamilton suddenly.

Burr lowered his pistol.

"What is the matter, General?" asked Pendleton.

Hamilton was squinting his eyes. It seemed as though he suddenly realized that he should not have chosen the side of the dueling ground that faced the sun.

"In certain situations of light, one requires glasses," Hamilton said as he reached into his pocket. He pulled out a pair of eyeglasses and put them on with his free hand. Then he raised his pistol and pointed it in several directions, as if he was testing his aim.

While Hamilton was going through these maneuvers, the TTT buzzed in Isabel's pocket.

WHAT IS GOING ON? REPORT BACK ASAP.

Isabel had the TTT in her hand, but she ignored it.

Hamilton seemed satisfied with his vision now and

got into position once again.

"This will do," he said. "Now you may proceed."

Did Hamilton put on his glasses to improve his chances of hitting Burr, or to make sure that he *wouldn't* hit him? Was he sending a subtle message to Burr that he was going to throw away his shot? Or maybe he just stopped the duel to throw off Burr's rhythm. Nobody will ever know.

Either way, Aaron Burr glared at him. He didn't find Hamilton's little charade to be amusing.

Van Ness and Pendleton turned around, so they were facing away from the duelists. That way, they would be able to honestly claim in a court of law that they did not actually see any guns being fired. Unfortunately, it also meant they would not be able to see exactly what happened and pass it on for the historical record. But the Flashback Four would.

"Are both parties ready now?" Pendleton shouted over his shoulder.

"Present," said Aaron Burr.

"Present," said Alexander Hamilton.

Both men lifted their pistols slowly.

"I can't look!" whispered Isabel.

Hamilton raised his pistol a little higher and to the

side of his target. He pulled the trigger.

BANG!

A shower of sparks and smoke sprayed forward from the muzzle of Hamilton's gun. The bullet shot out and struck the limb of a cedar tree about twelve feet off the ground and four feet wide of Burr. It was obvious that Hamilton *had* "thrown away his shot." Burr smiled a little after he realized the bullet had whistled past him. Hamilton's gun was empty.

Burr pointed his pistol straight at Hamilton. That's when things got crazy.

"Wait! Stop!" someone shouted.

It was Isabel.

She jumped up from behind the fallen tree, her hands waving in the air. All eyes turned to face her.

"Isabel!" Luke shouted. "What are you doing?"

She jumped over the tree trunk, out into the open area of the dueling ground. Hamilton, Burr, Pendleton, and Van Ness looked at her, dumbfounded.

"Who are *you*?" Pendleton shouted.

"Get back, Isabel!" shouted David.

"Are you crazy?" hollered Julia. "You'll get yourself killed!"

All of the Flashback Four were up on their feet now.

There was no reason to hide anymore.

"I don't care!" yelled Isabel. "I can't take this! It's insane!"

She marched right to the middle of the dueling ground, between Hamilton and Burr.

"Young lady!" hollered Hamilton. "This is no place—"

"Seize her!" shouted William Van Ness.

Van Ness and Pendleton advanced toward Isabel.

"Don't you *touch* her!" Luke shouted at them.

"Shut up, *all* of you!" Isabel pleaded. She was in tears now. "Enough! Can't you see that dueling is stupid and barbaric?"

"How long have you been hiding behind that tree, young lady?" asked Van Ness.

"My friends and I have been watching you the whole time," Isabel replied.

"Where did you come from?" asked Pendleton.

"You wouldn't believe me if I told you," Isabel shouted. "Look, it doesn't matter where we came from! The important thing is, you don't have to *do* this! You are two intelligent men! You don't need guns! You can settle your differences peacefully!"

"General Hamilton referred to me as despicable,"

said Aaron Burr. "I have every right to defend my honor."

"Despicable?" shouted Isabel. "So you're going to shoot him over an *adjective*? Didn't you ever hear that sticks and stones may break my bones, but names will never hurt me?"

"I have never heard that," Burr said.

Judging by the looks on the faces of Hamilton, Pendleton, and Van Ness, *nobody* had heard that expression in 1804.

"Mr. Burr, you're the vice president of the United States, for goodness' sake!" shouted Isabel. "And you, Mr. Hamilton, you're one of the most famous Americans in history. Your picture is going to be on the ten-dollar bill! There's going to be a Broadway show about you!"

"Ten-dollar bill?" asked Pendleton. "Broadway show? The young woman is clearly insane."

"You are two great men!" Isabel continued. "Do you have any idea of how childish you look right now? Fighting over a silly *word*? You're being *ridiculous*!"

David and Luke climbed over the tree trunk to try and pull Isabel out of harm's way. But she pushed them back.

"Who are *they*?" asked Burr.

"Leave them out of this!" Isabel shouted. "The point is, if you shoot Mr. Hamilton now, it's cold-blooded murder, that's all it is! And I'm a witness! I'll testify in court that I saw you do it! So I'm *begging* you! Just stop all this silliness and go home! Nobody has to die here today! You're both honorable men!"

All eyes turned to Aaron Burr now. He was the only one with a bullet in his gun. Burr looked furious, glaring at Isabel. The rules of the duel, which had been so carefully worked out in advance, had been changed without his consent. He had never agreed to having these four witnesses involved.

"Is this another one of your little games, General Hamilton?" he barked. "Did you put the young lady up to this? Well, I'm not falling for your distractions. She's not going to testify against me, or *anybody.*"

Burr turned and pointed his gun at Isabel's head.

"No! Don't!" shouted Julia.

"*Eeeeek!*" screamed Isabel, instinctively putting her hands in front of her face.

"Grab the gun!" David yelled. He and Luke charged at Burr.

But it was too late. Burr pulled the trigger. A shower of sparks sprayed out of the muzzle.

"Oh, shoot!" Luke screamed.

The bullet flew out of Burr's gun. It would have hit Isabel right between the eyes, but she was shielding her face with her hands. And the TTT was in one hand.

The bullet ricocheted off the TTT.

Isabel was knocked backward from the impact. The TTT went flying out of her hand. She stumbled and fell.

"Isabel!" shouted Julia.

Julia, Luke, and David ran over to Isabel, on her back in the dirt.

"Are you okay?" David said, cradling her head.

Julia examined Isabel's clothes and skin looking for blood or a bullet hole.

"Where did it hit you?" she asked Isabel. "Where does it hurt?"

"I'm okay, I think," Isabel said, opening her eyes. "It must have bounced off the TTT."

There was an audible groan coming from the other side of the dueling ground. The Flashback Four turned around as one.

Alexander Hamilton was on the ground.

CHAPTER 19

I AM A DEAD MAN

THE BULLET HAD RICOCHETED OFF THE TTT, which was in Isabel's hand, and struck Hamilton in the abdominal area, just above his right hip. He let out a cry, and the pistol dropped from his hand. Hamilton rose up on his toes for a moment, jerking violently to the left. Then he toppled over. A bloodstain appeared instantly on his shirt.

Then it was pandemonium.

"No!" screamed Pendleton as he rushed to Hamilton's side. "Dr. Hosack! Dr. Hosack! Come quickly!"

The instant Hamilton hit the ground, Aaron Burr took a step toward him, as if to see if he was okay. His second, William Van Ness, stopped him.

"Don't," he said simply. Van Ness didn't want Burr to be at the "scene of the crime" any longer than necessary. He opened an umbrella he had brought specifically for this purpose and held it in front of Burr's face as he pulled the vice president away.

"But I must speak to him," protested Burr.

"That would be ill-advised, Colonel," Van Ness said, almost dragging Burr toward the dirt footpath they had taken to get up to the dueling ground. Burr stumbled, spraining his ankle so he had to throw an arm around Van Ness's shoulder as they hustled away. The two men disappeared into the bushes, heading for the boat that would take them back to Manhattan.

Aside from the shock of having somebody point a gun at her and fire it, Isabel seemed to be okay. No injuries. David, Luke, and Julia left her for the moment and rushed over to where Hamilton had fallen to see if they could do anything.

On the ground behind them, the TTT, bulletproof and still operational, buzzed.

IS THE DUEL OVER? DID YOU GET THE VIDEO? the message read. But nobody looked at it. There were more important things to worry about.

Hamilton groaned in pain. The bloodstain on his

shirt was getting larger. He could barely speak.

"I am a dead man," he mumbled.

"No, you will live, General!" Pendleton said optimistically, leaning over his fallen friend. "We need you!"

Pendleton dragged Hamilton over to a small, reddish-brown boulder and propped him up against it so he was sitting in the grass. The color had drained from Hamilton's face. His blood was staining his pants now. He closed his eyes. It looked like he was dead.

"Breathe," Julia told Hamilton, not really knowing what else to say. The rest of the Flashback Four gathered around, looking on helplessly.

Dr. Hosack came charging up the path, holding his doctor's bag. He must have passed Burr and Van Ness as they were leaving the scene.

"Has the general been hit?" he hollered.

As soon as the doctor saw Hamilton, he had the answer to his question.

"Who are these children?" the doctor shouted. "Give him air!"

The Flashback Four backed away as Dr. Hosack took a knife from his bag and sliced open Hamilton's shirt. There was blood all over his stomach. The doctor didn't seem to mind. He examined Hamilton carefully, probing him with his fingers.

By the way, reader, if this had happened in the twenty-first century, things would have obviously been completely different. Somebody would have immediately called 911 on a cell phone, which didn't exist in 1804. In minutes, an ambulance or a helicopter—which also didn't exist back then—would have arrived. Hamilton would have been rushed to a hospital, which *did* exist but didn't have X-ray equipment, modern medicines, or the last two hundred years' worth of medical knowledge. In all probability, Hamilton's life would have been saved.

On the other hand, if this had happened in the twenty-first century, Hamilton and Burr wouldn't have been there in the first place. They would have settled their differences in a courtroom instead of on a dueling ground.

"He has fractured a rib on the right side," Dr. Hosack said. "The bullet may have hit his liver or lodged in his spine. It did not hit his heart."

"Will he live?" asked Pendleton.

"I don't know," the doctor replied. "There is no pulse, no breathing."

He took a little glass bottle out of his bag. The label said "Spirits of Hartshorn," a liquid made mostly of ammonia. The doctor quickly rubbed it on Hamilton's face, lips, temples, neck, and hands. He tried to pour some of it into Hamilton's closed mouth. Then he waved some smelling salts under his nose.

Miraculously, Hamilton opened his eyes and saw Hosack leaning over him.

"This is . . . a mortal wound, doctor," Hamilton said, closing his eyes again. He seemed semiconscious.

"Just rest," the doctor told him. "Don't try to speak, General."

"I went to the field . . . determined . . . not to take *his* life," Hamilton said, gasping for breath with each word.

At that moment, William Van Ness came running back up the footpath.

"Will the general live?" asked Van Ness.

"It remains to be seen," said Dr. Hosack.

"I have no ill will . . . ," Hamilton grunted, "against Colonel Burr. I met him . . . with a fixed resolution . . . to do him no harm. I forgive . . . all that happened."

"I will convey that message to him, General," said

Van Ness, and he hurried away again.

While the doctor was trying his best to clean out the wound, Hamilton opened his eyes again.

"I feel no feeling . . . in my legs," he mumbled. "When I am gone, please break the news gently to my dear wife, Eliza."

"You're not going anywhere, General," Dr. Hosack said. "There are more battles to be won."

That seemed to remind Hamilton of something. He looked around and saw his pistol lying on the ground about ten feet away.

"Be careful with that," he said. "It could discharge and injure someone." Hamilton was so out of it, he didn't realize he had already fired his gun.

"Let's get him to the boat," Dr. Hosack told Nathaniel Pendleton. The doctor grabbed Hamilton's upper body, and Pendleton took his legs. Together they lifted him up carried him toward the footpath.

"What can we do to help?" asked Isabel.

"Haven't you done enough already?" Pendleton barked without turning around.

He and Dr. Hosack rushed to carry Hamilton down the footpath and to the boat that would take them back to Manhattan. When they were gone, all was quiet on the dueling ground.

CHAPTER 20

DECISIONS, DECISIONS

ALEXANDER HAMILTON, AARON BURR, AND THEIR respective seconds had left Weehawken and were headed back across the river on separate boats. The sun was up now. None of the Flashback Four said anything for a long time. There was an eerie quiet on the dueling ground.

Finally, it was Luke who could no longer restrain himself. He ripped off the Hot Head and jammed it into his pocket.

"Are you insane?" he shouted at Isabel. "I can't believe you did that! What were you thinking?"

"Hey, easy, man," David said. "Give her a break."

"I couldn't help it!" Isabel said, almost in tears. "Something came over me. I couldn't bear the thought of Aaron Burr shooting a defenseless man. I'm sorry I did it."

"You almost got yourself killed!" Luke hollered.

"Forget about killed," said Julia. "We were specifically told not to interfere. And that's exactly what she did."

"Listen to *you*," David shouted at Julia. "*You're* the one who almost messed everything up when we were in Gettysburg and on the *Titanic*. You've got no right to criticize anybody."

"I didn't mess *anything* up on those missions," Julia protested. "Everything worked out fine. I didn't change history."

"Neither did Isabel," David said. "Hamilton was going to get shot no matter what any of us did."

"I said I was sorry," Isabel whimpered.

When something goes horribly wrong, there's a natural tendency to blame somebody. It's human nature. Emotions were running high. The Flashback Four needed to blow off some steam.

"I knew from the start that this mission was a dumb idea," Julia said. "We should have quit while we were ahead, after we got out of Pompeii."

"If I recall," David told her, "you were complaining that your life back home was boring after we got back from the Pompeii. Remember? Well, are you bored *now*?"

"Whose bright idea was this, anyway?" Luke asked.

"Not me," Isabel replied. "I didn't want to come here. I was perfectly happy being bored back home. I just went along with you guys."

"It was the Gunner's idea," said David. "*None* of us wanted to do this. She just about kidnapped us and tricked us into it."

"All we had to do was shoot the video and get out of here," Julia said. "That was the plan. You messed it up, Isabel. And *you're* the one who wanted that free ride to college so badly."

"Look, finger pointing isn't going to get us any-where," David told the others. "We all agreed to do this. Any one of us could have messed it up. And any one of us could have talked the others out of it. Some-times stuff just happens. So forget about it. The past doesn't matter anymore. Let's think about the future."

"You're right, dude," Luke said, calming down. "I'm sorry I yelled at you, Isabel."

"Me too," said Julia.

"It's okay," Isabel said, wiping her eyes.

The Flashback Four had a short group hug. Everybody tried to cool off and figure out what to do next. That's when they heard a quiet buzzing sound behind them.

"Oh no," they all said, turning around to look at the TTT lying in the grass.

"One more inch over and I'd be dead right now," Isabel said, going over to pick it up. "This little thing saved my life."

There was a small scrape on the TTT where Burr's bullet had bounced off, but otherwise it seemed as good as new.

"That Jones guy was right," Luke said. "That thing is indestructible."

Isabel flipped open the case. There were multiple texts on the screen, each one a few minutes apart . . .

IS IT OVER? DID YOU GET THE VIDEO?

DID YOU SHOOT THE VIDEO?

ANSWER PLEASE

DID YOU GET THE VIDEO? WHO SHOT FIRST? WHAT HAPPENED?

ARE YOU OK? ANSWER PLEASE!

"What should I say?" Isabel asked.

"Don't say anything," David advised. "Don't tell her a thing. Let's make sure she brings us back safely before we tell her what happened."

"Good idea," agreed Luke. "Let's get out of here."

Slowly, the Flashback Four made their way down the dirt footpath they had climbed to get up to the dueling ground. After a few anxious moments, they found their little rowboat where they had hidden it in the bushes. They climbed aboard, with the boys handling the oars, Julia in the front, and Isabel in the back. As soon as they pushed off into the water, the TTT buzzed again.

"Just ignore it," Julia said. "We need to think."

"I have to say *something*," Isabel replied. "If I don't, she might think we're dead."

Isabel typed this . . .

IT'S OVER. WE ARE ROWING BACK ACROSS THE RIVER NOW. WILL LET YOU KNOW WHEN WE GET TO NY.

Almost instantly, a reply came back . . .

DID YOU GET THE VIDEO?

To that, Isabel didn't reply. She closed the case of the TTT. The boys settled into the rhythm of the oars pulling through the water. All four of them were thinking about what had just happened in Weehawken.

"I killed Alexander Hamilton," Isabel finally said. "It was all my fault."

"Stop it," David told her. "He was going to die anyway. You know that. Burr would have shot him if we hadn't been there. Don't beat yourself up over it."

Luke stopped rowing for a moment.

"Hey, I just thought of something," he said. "What if Hamilton *doesn't* die?"

"What do you mean?" asked Julia. "Everybody knows he died. It's in the historical record."

"He died when Burr shot him *originally*," Luke told her. "But *this* time Hamilton didn't take a direct hit. The bullet ricocheted off the TTT. Maybe it didn't do as much damage when it hit him. Maybe he'll survive."

"Do you *really* think that could happen?" Isabel said hopefully. "That would be great!"

"No, it wouldn't," David countered. "If Hamilton lives, we will have changed history. Then we'll be in *real* trouble when we get home. We were specifically instructed not to change history."

"Still, I hope he lives," Isabel said. "I can't hope that he's going to die. That would be wrong."

"Well, for our sake, it would be better if he died," Luke said. "I'm just saying."

"Whatever happens to him," Isabel said ruefully, "I played a part in it. I'll have to live with that."

Meanwhile, Alexander Hamilton was in extreme pain, lying across the bottom of a boat that was being rowed furiously back to Manhattan. It had seemed like he was dead at first, but he revived when Dr. Hosack treated him with a reddish-brown painkiller called laudanum. It was made of opium, morphine, and codeine. In those days, laudanum was used as a home remedy for just about any ailment.

When the boat docked in Manhattan, Hamilton was carried to the mansion of his friend William Bayard and taken to a bedroom on the second floor. Rumors and gossip swirled immediately as the news spread about the duel. Somebody went to get Hamilton's wife, Eliza, from her home in Harlem, but it would take hours for her to get downtown. She would only be told that her husband had suffered "spasms."

Aaron Burr's boat docked in Manhattan before Hamilton's did. It has been said that when he arrived home, he laughed and threw a party to celebrate his victory in the duel. That may or may not have been true. Later, Burr would say that if his vision hadn't been impaired by the morning mist, he would have shot Hamilton in the heart. He didn't do himself any favors when it came to public opinion.

By the time the Flashback Four reached the middle of the Hudson River, the kids realized that some decisions had to be made. There was no way for them to look at the video Luke had shot with the Hot Head. It was stored on a chip. But they knew what had happened. What Luke had seen with his eyes was what he had filmed. Ms. Gunner and the folks at NOYB would not be happy to see that Isabel had interfered with the duel.

Luke stopped rowing and took the Hot Head out of his pocket. David stopped rowing also.

"We can't let them see the video," Luke stated plainly. "They'll go crazy if they know what happened back there."

"Agreed," said the others.

"We can't show it to *anybody*," added David.

"What we saw is our secret," said Julia. "*Forever.* Agreed?"

"Agreed," said the others.

"I vow to you guys right now that I will *never* tell what happened," David said. "They can torture me. They can do anything to me. I'll never tell."

"Agreed."

"We could hide the Hot Head," Isabel suggested.

"I don't even think we should bring it back with us," Luke said. "If we do, somebody will eventually get their hands on it."

"Then what should we do with it?" asked Isabel.

"We're going to have to destroy it," said David.

"How?" asked Julie. "The Hot Head is probably made out of the same stuff as the TTT. There's no way to destroy it."

"They probably spent a million dollars on the technology," said Isabel.

"Maybe more."

"I know how to destroy it," Luke said. "It's simple."

With that, he flipped the Hot Head over the side of the boat and into the river. The Flashback Four watched as it disappeared into the water.

CHAPTER 21

TRUTH AND LIES

BY THE TIME THEY GOT TO THE OTHER SIDE OF the river, David's and Luke's shoulders were aching. The current had picked up a bit, which made the rowing even harder.

"We're gonna have to do some serious lying when we see the Gunner," David told the others as the rowboat neared the dock. "You realize that, don't you?"

"I don't like to lie," Isabel replied.

"If we lie, she's going to be mad," Luke said. "But if we tell the truth, she's going to be *furious*."

"Remember what happened when Miss Z told the

truth about our pictures in her museum?" David said. "If she had only lied, none of this would have happened."

"Sometimes you *have* to lie," Julia said.

As the boat approached the little dock on the New York side, a figure was standing there—Benjamin Franklin Washington, the guy who'd sold them the rowboat.

"Well, well, well," he said. "I sure didn't 'spect to see you folks again."

"Here's your boat back, sir," Julia said as Benjamin Franklin Washington helped her step onto the dock. "Good as new. Thank you for letting us use it."

The boys stowed the oars and climbed onto the dock.

"Have a nice ride?" Benjamin Franklin Washington asked, looking them over carefully.

"Yes, it was lovely," Isabel told him as she let him help her out of the boat.

"Where did you go?" Benjamin Franklin Washington asked.

"Oh, you know," David replied, "around."

"Around . . . Weehawken, maybe . . . to watch the duel?"

The Flashback Four didn't reply. This Benjamin

Franklin Washington guy could be trouble. They didn't want anything to get in the way of their return trip home.

"Allow me to ask you a question," Benjamin Franklin Washington said. "How did you know there was going to be a duel up in those cliffs this mornin'?"

The kids shot glances at one another. Somebody had to step forward and be the group spokesperson. As usual, it was Luke.

"I'm really sorry," he said, "but we can't tell you how we knew. It's kind of a secret. You wouldn't believe us anyway."

"Did you witness it?" Benjamin Franklin Washington asked. "Did you see General Hamilton and the vice president?"

"Yeah, we saw them," Luke replied.

"Can you perchance tell me what transpired?" asked Benjamin Franklin Washington. "There are many rumors goin' around."

"Burr shot him," Luke said, glancing at Isabel. "It was as simple as that. Nothing more to say."

"Is Alexander Hamilton still alive?" asked Isabel anxiously.

"Far as I know, yes," Benjamin Franklin Washington told her. "But he may not make it through the day.

That's what people are sayin', anyway. Nobody knows for sure. Lotta gossip in the air this mornin'."

While Benjamin Franklin Washington tied his boat to the dock, Isabel turned her back on him so she could take the TTT out of her pocket. She typed in a quick text to Ms. Gunner . . .

WE ARE BACK AT THE DROP OFF POINT IN NY. GET US OUT OF HERE ASAP.

The reply came back in seconds . . .

OKAY. GET READY. NEED 1 MINUTE.

The Flashback Four gathered together in a tight clump.

"What's that yer doin'?" asked Benjamin Franklin Washington.

"Oh, this is just something that we do," Julia told him. "It's kind of our thing."

"That is an odd thing to do," he replied.

"Oh, you ain't seen nothin' yet," said David.

At NOYB headquarters in Boston, Ms. Gunner was sitting at the computer. Her old sidekick Jones was gone, but her team of nerdy-looking engineers was gathered around her. It looked like NASA headquarters in every movie you've seen about the space program.

Ms. Gunner had a scowl on her face. The Flash-back Four had ignored most of her texts, and they had refused to say whether or not they'd shot the video of the duel. She was used to having her orders followed. But there was nothing she could do. The situation was out of her control. Working with children was new to her.

"Okay, it's time, guys," she said to the group around the computer. "Let's bring those kids back."

One of the engineers flipped the switch on the Board to warm it up. Ms. Gunner typed a few commands on the keyboard and hit the ENTER key. Everyone looked at the Board expectantly.

Nothing happened.

"It's not working," somebody said nervously. "Something's wrong."

There was a lot of tension in the room. NOYB had successfully managed to send the Flashback Four to 1804, but none of the engineers were quite sure if they would be able to bring the group back.

"Do we have the correct date, time, latitude, longitude?" asked Ms. Gunner.

"Check."

They all looked at the Board again. Nothing.

"Those kids may be stuck there," one of the engineers said. "I knew this technology was kludgy."

"Nobody will ever know what happened," mumbled another one. "Our hands are clean."

"Stop that talk," barked Ms. Gunner. "You guys give up too easily."

There was a sudden buzzing sound, and then the screen on the Board lit up. A sigh of relief swept through the room. Five bands of color appeared across the Board. They shimmered for a few seconds, and then combined together into a band of intense white light.

"I just *felt* something!" Julia said excitedly.

"It's happening," said Luke.

"What the heck is goin' on?" asked Benjamin Franklin Washington, staring at them cluelessly. "Will you be needing me to summon a doctor?"

"Hopefully not," David assured him. "In a few seconds, this is gonna get a little weird. You might want to shield your eyes. Don't freak out."

Benjamin Franklin Washington had no idea what freaking out meant. But it didn't matter. A crackling sound filled the air around Isabel, Luke, David, and

Julia. They froze in place. It was like they had been gripped by a powerful invisible force. They held one another's hands tightly for support.

In Boston, a coffee cup vibrated on Ms. Gunner's desk.

"This is it," she said. "Here they come."

The bright white light stretched out and away from the surface of the Board until it came to a point three feet in front of it, like a laser beam. The humming sound intensified. Then there was an image, almost like a floating hologram. It was flickering. At first, it was impossible to make out any details.

The Flashback Four were flickering in the air now like a strobe light. Bits and pieces of David, Luke, Isabel, and Julia were illuminated. Then the Board began to pull them in, atom by atom, molecule by molecule. They were being digitally uploaded from the nineteenth century to the twenty-first, hopscotching the twentieth century entirely. The Board was struggling to fuse them into one complete picture.

"Holy—"

On the dock in New York City, Benjamin Franklin Washington stared, openmouthed. He had never seen anything like it. One moment these four kids were standing right in front of him, and the next moment, an explosion of light and smoke filled the air. A moment after that, they were gone. Benjamin Franklin Washington was left standing on the dock all by himself.

"Well," he said, "ain't that just about the dangest thing I've ever seen."

There was an explosion of light and smoke in Boston, too. Luke, Isabel, Julia, and David appeared in the flesh a few feet in front of the Board. They fell into the room, coughing and stumbling, flailing as they tumbled onto the carpet, knocking over a trash can and spilling its contents across the floor. They gasped for breath, happy, relieved, worn out, and emotional.

The Flashback Four was back.

NOYB headquarters erupted into raucous jubilation. The engineers were all whooping, hollering, high-fiving, slapping one another on the back, lighting cigars, and popping champagne corks.

"We made it!" David said, kissing the floor.

Ms. Gunner was the first one to welcome them, rushing over to help the kids off the floor and brush them off.

"Congratulations!" she said, smiling widely. "We

weren't sure you were going to make it for a minute there."

"Neither were we," Luke said. "It was touch and go."

Ms. Gunner was not one to waste time making small talk. She was all business.

"So," she said, holding out her hand, "may I have the Hot Head?"

"Don't you want to make sure we're okay?" asked Julia.

"You appear to be just fine," Ms. Gunner said brusquely. "We're all anxious to see the video. May I have the Hot Head?"

Luke, Julia, David, and Isabel looked at one another.

"Wow, you don't waste a minute, do you?" Luke said. "Don't you want to know what happened?"

"I'll know what happened when I've had the chance to review the video you made," she told him, holding out her hand again. "You *did* shoot the video, didn't you? Give it to me. Give me the Hot Head."

"I . . . we . . . don't have it," Luke admitted.

All traces of a smile were gone from Ms. Gunner's face now.

"Step into my office," she commanded. *"Now."*

The Flashback Four followed her into a small office. She slammed the door behind them and locked it.

"What do you *mean* you don't have it?" she demanded of Luke. "How can you not have it? It was strapped to your head!"

"It . . . came off," he said, still technically telling the truth.

"Where *is* it?" Ms. Gunner demanded with anger in her voice.

"It's . . . in the Hudson River," said Julia, also sticking with the truth.

"You have *got* to be kidding me," Ms. Gunner said, pounding her fist against the desk.

"It was an accident," Luke explained.

Okay, now the lying had begun.

"You let it fall into the *water*?" Ms. Gunner asked, incredulous. "And you just *left* it there? It was waterproof! Why didn't you dive in and get it out? Do you have any idea how much money the Hot Head is worth?"

"We're sorry," David said pointlessly.

The Gunner was fuming now, pacing the little office, trying to figure out what to do next. Her mind was racing. Maybe she could arrange to have the Hot Head fished out of the Hudson *now*, she thought. After all, it was still in the river, at the bottom somewhere. But that would be a very expensive operation, and the chances of finding it and having it survive over two hundred years underwater were tiny.

How would she explain this to her superiors? They would cut the funding for her program for sure. She might get fired. Everybody had high hopes for this mission.

Finally, her curiosity got the better of her.

"So, what happened in Weehawken?" she asked. "Did Hamilton shoot at all? Was he aiming at Burr? Who shot first? What did Burr do after Hamilton fell?" The questions tumbled out, one after the other.

"We . . . don't know what happened," Luke lied. "It was all kind of a blur."

Ms. Gunner had had it with these kids. Now she exploded.

"You don't know what happened?" she shouted, pushing Luke in the chest. "*That's* the best you can tell me? Why do you think we sent you back to 1804? Just for the *fun* of it? Did you think this was a little school field trip? A joyride? This was *important*! We chose you because you had experience with this. You supposedly knew what to do. We made it as simple as possible for you!"

"It all happened so fast," Isabel said lamely. "We just—"

"I *knew* I shouldn't have trusted a bunch of kids to get the job done," Ms. Gunner said. "Well, you can forget about those college scholarships. None of you deserve to go to college. You disgust me. Get out of here."

Hanging their heads, the Flashback Four moved toward the doorway.

"Can I ask you just one question?" Isabel said before opening the door.

"What is it?"

"Did Alexander Hamilton die in the duel?"

"Of *course* he died in the duel!" Ms. Gunner shouted at her. "We knew that already! That's *all* we knew. Why would you ask such a stupid question?"

"No reason," Isabel said meekly.

"Get out of my office!" Ms. Gunner shouted. "I don't want to see any of you ever again!"

CHAPTER 22

THE LAST GOOD-BYE

AND THAT, READERS, WAS THE END OF THE FLASH-back Four.

They had a pretty good run there, wouldn't you say? Four missions completed safely, and in two of them—*Titanic* and Pompeii—the kids brought back the photos they had been assigned to shoot. While it's true that they had failed to deliver the goods at Gettysburg and Weehawken, they were still batting .500. Not too shabby.

But it was over. Done. Finished. The Flashback Four were now just Luke, Isabel, Julia, and David. They would never travel through time again.

Oh, wait, reader. Just one more little thing. I almost forgot . . .

A couple of Saturdays after the "Weirdness in Weehawken," as they called it, the kids were back to their normal lives. David was shooting hoops with his friends at the park that day. Julia was shopping. Isabel was at the library catching up on some schoolwork. Luke was playing pinball.

Each of the Flashback Four was lost in his or her own private world, when four men in identical dark suits approached them individually.

"Excuse me," the man whispered to Isabel, "I'm sorry to bother you. Are you Isabel Alvarez?"

"Yes," she replied, alarmed. "Is something wrong?"

The man didn't respond. He simply reached into his jacket pocket and handed Isabel a yellow enve-lope. Then he turned on his heel and walked away. The same thing happened to David, Luke, and Julia.

For a moment, Isabel was confused. Then she remembered—a yellow envelope. That was how she got involved with the Flashback Four to begin with. It felt like a long time ago when a mysterious stranger had handed her a yellow envelope inviting her to a "very special once-in-a-lifetime experience" at the Hancock Building in downtown Boston. Twenty dollars had been clipped to the invitation the first time.

Quickly, Isabel tore open the envelope. There was no money inside, but there was a note . . .

Come to 75 Francis Street, Boston, Massachusetts, as soon as possible. Please do not share this or discuss it with anyone.

There was no signature and no return address. Isabel quickly gathered up her books and stuffed them into her backpack. She checked the address on her smartphone. Francis Street was less than a mile away. She could walk it.

The sign above the awning at 75 Francis Street said BRIGHAM AND WOMEN'S HOSPITAL. It didn't take long for Isabel to put two and two together—Miss Z must be here. She was dying. She probably wanted to say her last good-byes.

Isabel hurried through the automatic doors and walked over to the information desk.

"May I help you?" the receptionist asked.

"I received this envelope," Isabel replied, taking it

out of her backpack.

"Oh, yes. Room 333. The elevators are behind you."

Isabel took the elevator up to the third floor and found the right room. Mrs. Vader was standing outside the door, dabbing her eyes with a tissue. Isabel gave her a hug, which only made the two of them more emotional.

"She's dying, isn't she?" asked Isabel.

"Yes," Mrs. Vader said. "It won't be long now."

"May I see her?"

"Of course."

Isabel was ushered into the hospital room. Luke, David, and Julia were already there, standing quietly and respectfully at one side of the bed. They nodded at Isabel when she came in. The mood was somber. There were some flowers on the windowsill, along with framed photographs the kids had taken of Mount Vesuvius and the *Titanic*. Soft music was playing in the background.

Miss Z was asleep. Her hair was stringy, and her skin looked more pale than usual. She seemed so fragile, lying there. It looked like she was already dead. No words were spoken for some time.

"This is what it's like when somebody dies, huh?"

asked Luke. "I've never seen anybody die."

"I did," said David. "My grandpa."

Julia couldn't speak at all. She held a tissue against her face.

"Is she conscious?" asked Isabel.

"She fades in and out," replied Mrs. Vader. "One minute she seems perfectly lucid, and then it looks like she's barely alive. Even if she seems like she's out of it, she told me that she wanted the four of you to come here today."

Isabel went over and knelt at Miss Z's bedside. She recited a prayer silently.

"I don't know if you can hear me," Isabel said quietly, "but I never took the time to thank you for the wonderful experiences you gave me. Experiences you gave *all* of us. The memories are starting to fade, but the photographs will always be there. I will try really hard not to forget what we did together. Thank you for giving me the opportunity."

The Flashback Four were all in tears now. Even Luke was wiping his face with his sleeve.

That's when Miss Z opened her eyes. Isabel was so startled, she almost fell over. Mrs. Vader looked relieved.

"Knock it off," Miss Z said to the kids. "I'm not dead yet. Not by a long shot. Stop that whimpering."

"It's so good to see you and hear the sound of your voice!" David said. "I thought you were being held prisoner or something."

"I was," Miss Z replied. "But I guess they just figured the old lady is going to die any day, so I'm no threat to them anymore. I'm no use to them either, so they just decided to let me go in peace. Stopped harassing me. Real humanitarians, huh?"

"How long do you have?" Luke asked.

"Luke! You don't ask questions like that!" said Julia, exasperated.

"What did I say?" asked Luke innocently.

"Who knows how long I have?" said Miss Z. "It could be days. It could be weeks."

That set off another round of sobbing.

"Look, I didn't invite you kids here to slobber all over yourselves," Miss Z said. "I need you to do something. That's why I called you in here. Mrs. Vader?"

Mrs. Vader left the room for a moment. When she returned, she was wheeling in a large smartboard.

"Is that . . . what I *think* it is?" asked Isabel.

"It sure is," replied Miss Z.

"It's the Board!" exclaimed Luke.

"How did you get it back?" David asked. "They took it from you."

"I *didn't* get it back," Miss Z told them. "I built two of them, in case of emergency. Let that be a lesson to you. Always back up your work, in case you lose your first copy."

Mrs. Vader left the room again and came back in wheeling a computer on a cart.

"Wait," said Julia. "Are you . . . going to send us somewhere?"

"No," Miss Z replied. "You're going to send *me* somewhere. It's my turn now."

The Flashback Four unleashed a flurry of questions. "What? Where? When? Why?"

"Calm down," Miss Z told them. "Look, you know my situation. Many wonderful researchers have been working for a long time, but they haven't found a cure for ALS. I've been waiting my whole adult life. Now I'm running out of time."

Isabel, David, Luke, and Julia stared at her, in varying degrees of comprehension.

"Do I have to spell it out for you?" Miss Z finally told them. "They may find a cure for my ALS one day in the future. So that's where I want you to send me. To the future."

"Wow!" Luke said, finally getting it. "So when you get to the future, maybe the doctors there can like, give you a shot or a pill or something and you'll be all better?"

"That's what I'm hoping," said Miss Z.

"Let's *do* it!" David shouted excitedly.

"Yeah!" yelled the others.

The Flashback Four rolled Miss Z's bed over so that it was as close as possible to the Board. Julia flipped on the switch to warm it up. Mrs. Vader plugged in the computer, turned it on, and checked the connection to make sure the computer and the Board were communicating with each other wirelessly. The Board buzzed, clicked, and flashed random letters and numbers as it warmed up.

"Let's make sure there are no screw-ups this time," Luke said, taking a seat at the computer next to Isabel. "First we need to set the date."

"When do you want to arrive?" asked Isabel.

"I was thinking a hundred years into the future," said Miss Z.

"Check," Isabel said, typing on the keyboard. "Date is set. A hundred years from today."

"Next, we need to put in the time of day," said Luke.

"It doesn't matter," Miss Z told them. "Anytime."

"Twelve noon?" asked Isabel.

"Sure," said Miss Z. "Maybe they'll give me lunch when I arrive."

"Check," Isabel said. "Time of day is set. Noon."

"Latitude and longitude next," said Luke. "What should we put in? Where do you want to go, exactly?"

"Right here, at the hospital," said Miss Z. "Don't change a thing."

"Let's hope this hospital is still here a hundred years from now," said David. "If not, whoever lives here is going to get a big surprise."

"Check," said Isabel. "Current latitude and longitude are locked in."

The Board flashed three times, and then five bands of color appeared.

"You ready?" asked David.

"Ready as I'll ever be," replied Miss Z.

"Nervous?" asked Julia.

"Of *course* I'm nervous!" said Miss Z. "Wouldn't *you* be? I'm going to be starting a new life in a new time."

Isabel clicked the mouse a few times.

"Remember," David told Miss Z, "you're not going there to sightsee or get souvenirs."

Nobody laughed until David added, "Just kidding!"

"Okay, do it, Isabel," instructed Luke.

Isabel typed the last few commands into the keyboard. When she hit the ENTER key, there was a short buzzing sound. The five bands of color flashed, and then there was an explosion of sound.

"It's working!" shouted Julia.

The five bands of color merged together to form one band of intense white light.

"Close your eyes, Miss Z!" Luke shouted.

The light jumped off the Board with a crackle and stretched away from the surface, toward Miss Z in her bed.

"It's beautiful!" she shouted.

Then the humming sound kicked in. Everything in the room was vibrating.

The band of white light had made a connection with Miss Z's body. It was pulling her in.

"This is it!" yelled Luke.

"Brace yourself!" hollered Julia.

Miss Z started flickering.

"It's happening!" shouted Mrs. Vader. "Good-bye, Miss Zandergoth!"

"What are you going to do in the future?" asked Isabel.

"Time will tell," Miss Z replied.

There was one last flash of light, and a puff of smoke. The noise, the lights, and the vibrations came to a halt. Everything was quiet.

Miss Z was gone.

FACTS & FICTIONS

Everything in this book is true, except for the stuff I made up. It's only fair to tell you which is which.

First, the made-up stuff. The Flashback Four, Miss Z, and the Gunner do *not* exist. There's no secret government organization called NOYB (unless, of course, they really *do* exist but they're so secret that I don't know about them). While the Hot Head seems plausible, there's no such thing as a smartboard that will send people through time or a TTT to send texts through time. At least not yet.

Some of the dialogue in this book (like Hamilton and Burr on the dueling ground) was invented. Some of it was real, but it took place on the boat heading back to New York. And some of Hamilton's letters were written in the week *before* the last night of his life. Just about everything else concerning the Hamilton-Burr duel—the names, dates, times, locations, and so on, is true. Nathaniel Pendleton and Dr. Hosack *did* try to talk Hamilton out of dueling when they arrived to pick him up that fateful night.

To research this book, I scoured the internet for websites that discussed the Hamilton-Burr duel, watched videos about it, and went to Weehawken to see the site of the duel with my own eyes. (There's not much to see. Over the years, a number of monuments there have been vandalized or stolen by souvenir hunters.)

But mostly, I got the information from reading other books on the subject, for both children and adults. To name a few: *Alexander Hamilton* by Ron Chernow; *War of Two: Alexander Hamilton, Aaron Burr, and the Duel that Stunned the Nation* by John Sedgwick; *The Duel: The Parallel Lives of Alexander Hamilton and Aaron Burr* by Judith St. George; and *Affairs of Honor: National Politics in the New Republic* by Joanne B. Freeman. Hey, you think authors know all this stuff we write about? We look it up!

If you're fascinated by the story of the Hamilton-Burr duel—as so many people are—there's lots more information about it. Go to your local library. And there's tons of stuff online. I barely scratched the surface in this book. If you want to read *all* the gory details, well, that's why they invented Google. And of course, go see the show *Hamilton* if you can.

We'll never know for sure what happened that summer morning in Weehawken. Aaron Burr's second said Alexander Hamilton fired his gun first and simply missed. Hamilton's second said Burr fired first, and that Hamilton didn't shoot until after he was hit.

By the way, there's an interesting story about the pistols they used. They were supplied by Hamilton's brother-in-law John Church and remained in Church's family until 1930, when his granddaughter sold them to the Bank of the Manhattan—a bank founded by . . . wait for it . . . Aaron Burr! That bank eventually merged

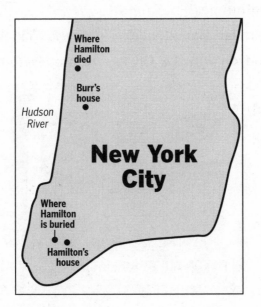

to become JP Morgan Chase, and the pistols are still in the company's archives today.

This is what we *do* know: After he was shot, Alexander Hamilton was rushed back across the river, and he survived the night. In the morning, his wife, Eliza, and their seven children were brought to his deathbed. Eliza fanned him and snipped a lock of his hair. Hamilton opened his eyes for a moment, looked at his family, and closed his eyes again. He could barely speak at that point, but he told his family that he had planned from the start to throw away his shot. Just two years earlier, Hamilton had given his son Philip that same advice before *his* duel. It was the same result both times.

Alexander Hamilton died at two o'clock in the afternoon on July 12, thirty-one hours after getting

shot. The bloodstains on the floor beneath his death-bed were left there for many years.

The news traveled fast in New York City, and there was an outpouring of grief much like when George Washington had died less than five years earlier. Another Founding Father had fallen, and this time it had been sudden and violent. Along the parade route to the funeral two days later, thousands of mourners lined the streets to pay their respects. Church bells pealed. Flags were flown at half-mast. Guns were fired. Hamilton was buried with full military honors at Trinity Church, not far from where he had lived, studied, and practiced law. (The church is just five blocks from the offices of HarperCollins, the publisher of this book.)

Eliza Hamilton lived another fifty years and died at the age of ninety-seven in 1854. Eliza crusaded against

slavery and helped start the first private orphanage in New York. She is buried next to her husband.

One good thing that came out of Alexander Hamilton's death was the decline of dueling in America. He was the most *famous* person to die in a duel, and the public demanded that anti-dueling laws be enforced. As a result, within a few decades, these "affairs of honor" had pretty much faded away.

What about Aaron Burr? After the duel, Burr was rowed back across the Hudson to a dock at Canal Street. From there, he went to his home, Richmond Hill, by horseback. It was almost like a day at the office.

But he hadn't realized how angry people would be that he had killed Alexander Hamilton. Burr was called an assassin in the newspapers. There were threats to burn his house down. He was indicted for murder by the state of New Jersey.

Even though he would still officially be the vice president of the United States for another eight months, Burr was forced to leave New York. He fled to Philadelphia, then to an island off the coast of Georgia, and then to Florida. Everywhere he went, he was scorned.

Burr headed west to Kentucky, Tennessee, Ohio,

and Mississippi. Somewhere along the line, he got the crazy idea to take over the Louisiana Territory (acquired by the United States in 1803) and form his own country there. President Thomas Jefferson found out about the plot, and in 1807 Aaron Burr was arrested and brought to trial for treason. He was acquitted, but he was considered a traitor by the public and a wanted man all over the United States. So he fled to Europe and lived there for four years, sometimes under a different name.

By 1812, America was at war with England (again!), and the United States government had little interest in pursuing Aaron Burr. So he sailed home to New York City and quietly began practicing law again. But it was one tragedy after another. First his granddaughter died. Then his daughter, Theodosia, died at sea on her way from South Carolina to visit him. She was only twenty-nine.

Burr became a recluse. Occasionally, he would get recognized on the street and attacked. In 1833, he married a wealthy widow named Eliza Jumel. The marriage didn't last. (The house Burr lived in with Eliza Jumel and Alexander Hamilton's home the Grange are both still standing today, one mile away from each other in Upper Manhattan.)

Burr never expressed much regret or remorse for killing Hamilton. The closest he ever came was at the end of his life, when he was quoted as saying, "I should have known the world was wide enough for both Hamilton and me."

In 1836, Aaron Burr died at the age of eighty in a Staten Island hotel. The third vice president of the United States was buried without ceremony in Princeton, New Jersey, a few feet from his father and grandfather.

Burr died in disgrace while Hamilton is remembered as an American hero, celebrated on our money and in Broadway theater. So historically speaking, it's fair to say that Hamilton, in fact, was the winner of the duel.

ABOUT THE AUTHOR

Besides Flashback Four, Dan Gutman is the author of the Genius Files series, the My Weird School series, the Baseball Card Adventure series, *Rappy the Raptor*, and many other books for young readers. He lives in New York City with his wife, Nina. You can find out more about Dan and his books if you visit www.dangutman.com.

READ THEM ALL!

A TIME-TRAVELING ADVENTURE UNLIKE ANY OTHER!

HARPER
An Imprint of HarperCollinsPublishers

www.harpercollinschildrens.com